Selected Stories by
WILKIE COLLINS

Books in this Series:

Selected Stories by O. Henry
Selected Stories by Anton Chekhov
Selected Stories by Guy de Maupassant
Selected Stories by Mark Twain
Selected Stories by Rudyard Kipling
Selected Stories by Leo Tolstoy
Selected Stories by Edgar Allan Poe
Selected Stories by Saki
Selected Stories by Oscar Wilde
Selected Stories by Honoré de Balzac
Selected Stories by Charles Dickens
Selected Stories by D.H. Lawrence
Selected Stories by H.G. Wells
Selected Stories by Jack London
Selected Stories by Joseph Conrad
Selected Stories by Sir Arthur Conan Doyle
Selected Stories by James Joyce
Selected Stories by Virginia Woolf
Selected Stories by Thomas Hardy
Selected Stories by Fyodor Dostoyevsky
Selected Stories by Katherine Mansfield
Selected Stories by Robert Louis Stevenson
Selected Stories by Howard Pyle
Selected Stories by Jerome K. Jerome
Selected Stories by Sir Walter Scott
Selected Stories by H. Rider Haggard
Selected Stories by G.K. Chesterton
Selected Stories by Bram Stoker
Selected Stories by Henry James
Selected Stories by F. Scott Fitzgerald
Selected Stories by W.W. Jacobs
Selected Stories by A.A. Milne
Selected Stories by Nathaniel Hawthorne
Selected Stories by Alexandre Dumas
Selected Essays by Charles Lamb

Selected Stories by
WILKIE COLLINS

Published by
Rupa Publications India Pvt. Ltd 2014
161-B/4, Gulmohar House,
Yusuf Sarai Community Centre,
New Delhi 110049

Sales centres:
Bengaluru Chennai
Hyderabad Kolkata Mumbai

Selection and Introduction copyright © Terry O'Brien 2014

All rights reserved.
No part of this publication may be reproduced, transmitted, or stored in a retrieval system, in any form or by any means, electronic, mechanical, photocopying, recording or otherwise, without the prior permission of the publisher.

P-ISBN: 978-81-291-3524-7
E-ISBN: 978-93-5333-933-3

Second impression 2025

10 9 8 7 6 5 4 3 2

Printed in India

This book is sold subject to the condition that it shall not, by way of trade or otherwise, be lent, resold, hired out, or otherwise circulated, without the publisher's prior consent, in any form of binding or cover other than that in which it is published.

CONTENTS

Introduction vii

1. Brother Owen's Story of the Siege of the Black Cottage 1
2. Brother Griffith's Story of the Family Secret 21
3. Farmer Fairweather 43
4. The Hidden Cash 51
5. Nine O'Clock 59
6. The Traveller's Story of a Terribly Strange Bed 82
7. The Twin Sisters: A True Story 102
8. The Last Stage Coachman 126

INTRODUCTION

William Wilkie Collins (8 January 1824–23 September 1889) was an English novelist, playwright, and author of short stories. His best known works are *The Woman in White, The Moonstone, Armadale,* and *No Name*. He was a master of detective fiction but he also wrote numerous essays, short stories and a dozen plays, and also published twenty-three novels. On 12 March 1851, Collins embarked on his lifelong love of the theatre when he was recruited to act in one of Charles Dickens' amateur theatre productions. He and Dickens, twelve years his senior, became great friends and collaborated on articles for Dickens' periodical *Household Words* and other journals.

- 'Brother Owen's Story of the Siege of the Black Cottage' begins with the heroine, Bessie, a stonemason's daughter acting as the narrator of her own tale. The main events take place when eighteen-year-old Bessie is left alone at night in an isolated cottage, and acts with exemplary courage and ingenuity to protect a large sum of money, left in her care by a wealthy neighbour, from a violent gang of ruffians.
- 'Brother Griffith's Story of the Family Secret' is a sad and heart-warming tale of a young man who seeks the truth about a family tragedy, 'a skeleton in the cupboard' as he calls it, that no one wants to talk about.

- 'Farmer Fairweather' is a brilliant commentary on the miscarriage of justice through the most petty of circumstances. The story begins with a woman looking for a job as a housekeeper who lands up at the doorstep of Farmer Fairweather. A misunderstanding of massive proportions leads her to lay a false accusation upon him.
- 'The Hidden Cash' is yet another tale of the erroneous mechanisms of justice provided by Victorian era courts. It tells the tale of an innocent man who is accused of murdering a traveller sleeping in his house; the case grows black against him simply because he cannot satisfactorily explain why he had hidden money in his own garden.
- 'Nine O'Clock' is a powerful French Revolution piece that combines clairvoyance with more traditional themes. On the night before their execution during the fated Revolution, twenty-one condemned prisoners and their friends are permitted a last banquet before their trip to the guillotine the next day. While they feast and jest, only one prisoner, Duprat, is quiet on the subject, and he proceeds to tell his friend about a family curse.
- 'The Traveller's Story of a Terribly Strange Bed' begins with two Englishmen who are travelling to the city of Paris, when they enter a gambling house. The narrator, after winning hugely and getting drunk, is persuaded by an old soldier to spend the night at the inn upstairs; however, the narrator discovers at night strange things happening around him, and his bed seems to be moving.
- 'The Twin Sisters: A True Story' is a fascinating tale which begins with a gentleman, Mr Streatfield, having come to attend the king's levées in London, when he comes across a face in a balcony that he immediately falls in love with. What ensues is a rather unusual love story with confusion of massive proportions.

- 'The Last Stage Coachman', one of Collins' most popular short stories, is an eerie tale of a way of life lost. The story is a supernatural allegory of trains, which deals with a simple theme like the ousting of the stagecoach by the railway, but colours it with supernatural visitations—such as that of a fully equipped stagecoach in the clouds.

1

BROTHER OWEN'S STORY OF THE SIEGE OF THE BLACK COTTAGE

To begin at the beginning, I must take you back to the time after my mother's death, when my only brother had gone to sea, when my sister was out at service, and when I lived alone with my father, in the midst of a moor in the west of England.

The moor was covered with great limestone rocks, and intersected here and there by streamlets. The nearest habitation to ours was situated about a mile and a half off, where a strip of the fertile land stretched out into the waste like a tongue. Here the outbuildings of the great Moor Farm, then in the possession of my husband's father, began. The farmlands stretched down gently into a beautiful rich valley, lying nicely sheltered by the high platform of the moor. When the ground began to rise again, miles and miles away, it led up to a country house called Holme Manor, belonging to a gentleman named Knifton. Mr Knifton had lately married a young lady whom my mother had nursed, and whose kindness and friendship for me, her foster-sister, I shall remember gratefully to the last day of my life. These and other slight particulars it is necessary to my story that I should tell you, and it is also necessary that you should be especially careful to bear them well in mind.

My father was by trade a stonemason. His cottage stood a mile and a half from the nearest habitation. In all other directions we were four or five times that distance from neighbours. Being very poor people, this lonely situation had one great attraction for us—we lived rent free on it. In addition to that advantage, the stones, by shaping which my father gained his livelihood, lay all about him at his very door; so that he thought his position, solitary as it was, quite an enviable one. I can hardly say that I agreed with him, though I never complained. I was very fond of my father, and managed to make the best of my loneliness with the thought of being useful to him. Mrs Knifton wished to take me into her service when she married, but I declined—unwillingly enough—for my father's sake. If I had gone away, he would have had nobody to live with him; and my mother made me promise on her deathbed that he should never be left to pine away alone in the midst of the bleak moor.

Our cottage, small as it was, was stoutly and snugly built, with stone from the moor as a matter of course. The walls were lined inside and fenced outside with wood, the gift of Mr Knifton's father to my father. This double covering of cracks and crevices, which would have been superfluous in a sheltered position, was absolutely necessary, in our exposed situation, to keep out the cold winds which, excepting just the summer months, swept over us continually all the year round. The outside boards, covering our roughly-built stone walls, my father protected against the wet with pitch and tar. This gave to our little abode a curiously dark, dingy look, especially when it was seen from a distance; and so it had come to be called in the neighbourhood, even before I was born, The Black Cottage.

I have now related the preliminary particulars which it is desirable that you should know, and may proceed at once to the pleasanter task of telling you my story.

One cloudy autumn day, when I was rather more than eighteen years old, a herdsman walked over from Moor Farm with a letter which had been left there for my father. It came from a builder living at our county town, half a day's journey off, and it invited my father to come to him and give his judgment about an estimate for some stonework on a very large scale. My father's expenses for loss of time were to be paid, and he was to have his share of employment afterwards in preparing the stone. He was only too glad, therefore, to obey the directions which the letter contained, and to prepare at once for his long walk to the county town.

Considering the time at which he received the letter, and the necessity of resting before he attempted to return, it was impossible for him to avoid being away from home for one night, at least. He proposed to me, in case I disliked being left alone in the Black Cottage, to lock the door and to take me to Moor Farm to sleep with any of the milkmaids who would give me a share of her bed. I by no means liked the notion of sleeping with a girl whom I did not know, and I saw no reason to feel afraid of being left alone for only one night; so I declined. No thieves had ever come near us; our poverty was sufficient protection against them; and of other dangers there were none that even the most timid person could apprehend. Accordingly, I got my father's dinner, laughing at the notion of my taking refuge under the protection of a milkmaid at Moor Farm. He started for his walk as soon as he had done, saying he should try and be back by dinner-time the next day, and leaving me and my cat Polly to take care of the house.

I had cleared the table and brightened up the fire, and had sat down to my work with the cat dozing at my feet, when I heard the trampling of horses, and, running to the door, saw Mr and Mrs Knifton, with their groom behind them, riding up to the Black Cottage. It was part of the young lady's kindness never to neglect an opportunity of coming to pay me a friendly visit, and her husband was generally willing to accompany her for his wife's sake. I made my best curtsey, therefore, with a great deal of pleasure, but with no particular surprise at seeing them. They dismounted and entered the cottage, laughing and talking in great spirits. I soon heard that they were riding to the same county town for which my father was bound and that they intended to stay with some friends there for a few days, and to return home on horseback, as they went out.

I heard this, and I also discovered that they had been having an argument, in jest, about money-matters, as they rode along to our cottage. Mrs Knifton had accused her husband of inveterate extravagance, and of never being able to go out with money in his pocket without spending it all, if he possibly could, before he got home again. Mr Knifton had laughingly defended himself by declaring that all his pocket-money went in presents for his wife, and that, if he spent it lavishly, it was under her sole influence and superintendence.

'We are going to Cliverton now,' he said to Mrs Knifton, naming the county town, and warming himself at our poor fire just as pleasantly as if he had been standing on his own grand hearth. 'You will stop to admire every pretty thing in every one of the Cliverton shop-windows; I shall hand you the purse, and you will go in and buy. When we have reached home again, and you have had time to get tired of your purchases, you will clasp your hands in amazement, and declare that you are quite shocked at my habits of extravagance. I am only the banker who keeps the money—you, my love, are the spendthrift who throws it all away!'

'Am I, sir?' said Mrs Knifton, with a look of mock indignation. 'We will see if I am to be misrepresented in this way with impunity. Bessie, my dear' (turning to me), 'you shall judge how far I deserve the character which my husband has just given to me. *I* am the spendthrift, am I? And you are only the banker? Very well. Banker, give me my money at once, if you please!'

Mr Knifton laughed, and took some gold and silver from his waistcoat pocket.

'No, no,' said Mrs Knifton. 'You may want what you have got there for necessary expenses. Is that all the money you have about you? What do I feel here?' and she tapped her husband on the chest, just over the breast-pocket of his coat.

Mr Knifton laughed again, and produced his pocketbook. His wife snatched it out of his hand, opened it, and drew out some banknotes, put them back again immediately, and closing the pocketbook, stepped across the room to my poor mother's little walnut-wood bookcase—the only bit of valuable furniture we had in the house.

'What are you going to do there?' asked Mr Knifton, following his wife.

Mrs Knifton opened the glass door of the bookcase, put the pocketbook in a vacant place on one of the lower shelves, closed and locked the door again, and gave me the key.

'You called me a spendthrift just now,' she said. 'There is my answer. Not one farthing of that money shall you spend at Cliverton on *me*. Keep the key in your pocket, Bessie, and, whatever Mr Knifton may say, on no account let him have it until we call again on our way back. No, sir, I won't trust you with that money in your pocket in the town of Cliverton. I will make sure of your taking it all home again, by leaving it here in more trustworthy hands than yours, until we ride back. Bessie, my dear, what do you say to that, as a lesson in economy inflicted on a prudent husband by a spendthrift wife?'

She took Mr Knifton's arm while she spoke, and drew him away to the door. He protested, and made some resistance, but she easily carried her point, for he was far too fond of her to have a will of his own in any trifling matter between them. Whatever the men might say, Mr Knifton was a model husband in the estimation of all the women who knew him.

'You will see us as we come back, Bessie. Till then, you are our banker, and the pocketbook is yours,' cried Mrs Knifton gaily, at the door. Her husband lifted her into the saddle, mounted himself, and away they both galloped over the moor, as wild and happy as a couple of children.

Although my being trusted with money by Mrs Knifton was no novelty (in her maiden days she always employed me to pay her dressmaker's bills), I did not feel quite easy at having a pocketbook full of banknotes left by her in my charge. I had no positive apprehension about the safety of the deposit placed in my hands, but it was one of the odd points in my character then (and I think it is still) to feel an unreasonably strong objection to charging myself with money responsibilities of any kind, even to suit the convenience of my dearest friends. As soon as I was left alone, the very sight of the pocketbook behind the glass door of the bookcase began to worry me; and, instead of returning to my work, I puzzled my brains about finding a place to lock it up in, where it would not be exposed to the view of any chance passer-by, who might stray into the Black Cottage.

This was not an easy matter to compass in a poor house like ours, where we had nothing valuable to put under lock and key. After running over various hiding-places in my mind, I thought of my tea-caddy, a present of Mrs Knifton's, which I always kept out of harm's way in my own bedroom. Most unluckily—as it afterwards turned out—instead of taking the pocketbook to the tea-caddy, I went into my room first, to take the tea-caddy to the pocketbook. I only acted in this roundabout way from sheer thoughtlessness, and severely enough I was punished for it, as you will acknowledge yourself when you have read a page or two more of my story.

I was just getting the unlucky tea-caddy out of my cupboard, when I heard footsteps in the passage, and running out immediately, saw two men walk into the kitchen—the room in which I had received Mr and Mrs Knifton. I enquired what they wanted, sharply enough, and one of them answered immediately that they wanted my father. He turned towards me, of course, as he spoke, and I recognized him as a stonemason, going among his comrades by the name of Shifty Dick. He bore a very bad character for everything but wrestling—a sport for which the working men of our parts were famous all through the county. Shifty Dick was champion, and he had got his name from some tricks in wrestling, for which he was celebrated. He was a tall, heavy man, with a lowering, scarred face, and huge hairy hands—the last visitor in the whole world that I should have been glad to see under any circumstances. His companion was a stranger, whom he addressed by the name of Jerry—a quick, dapper, wicked-looking man, who took off his cap to me with mock politeness, and showed, in so doing, a very bald head, with some very ugly-looking knobs on it. I distrusted him worse than I did Shifty Dick, and managed to get between his leering eyes and the bookcase, as I told the two that my father was gone out, and that I did not expect him back till the next day.

The words were hardly out of my mouth before I repented that my anxiety to get rid of my unwelcome visitors had made me incautious enough to acknowledge that my father would be away from home for the whole night.

Shifty Dick and his companion looked at each other when I unwisely let out the truth, but made no remark, except to ask me if I would give them a drop of cider. I answered, sharply, that I had no cider in the house—having no fear of the consequences of refusing them drink, because I knew that plenty of men were at work within hail, in a neighbouring quarry. The two looked at each other again when I denied having any cider to give them; and Jerry (as I am obliged to call him, knowing no other name by which to distinguish the fellow) took off his cap to me once more, and, with a kind of blackguard gentility upon him, said they would have the pleasure of calling the next day, when my father was at home. I said good afternoon as ungraciously as possible, and, to my great relief, they both left the cottage immediately afterwards.

As soon as they were well away, I watched them from the door. They trudged off in the direction of Moor Farm; and, as it was beginning to get dusk, I soon lost sight of them.

Half an hour afterwards I looked out again.

The wind had lulled with the sunset, but the mist was rising and a heavy rain was beginning to fall. Never did the lonely prospect of the moor look so dreary as it looked to my eyes that evening. Never did I regret any slight thing more sincerely than I then regretted the leaving of Mr Knifton's pocketbook in my charge. I cannot say that I suffered under any actual alarm, for I felt next to certain that neither Shifty Dick nor Jerry had got a chance of setting eyes on so small a thing as the pocketbook, while they were in the kitchen; but there was a kind of vague distrust troubling me—a suspicion of the night—a dislike at being left by myself, which I never remember having experienced before. This feeling so increased, after I had closed the door and gone back to the kitchen, that, when I heard the voices of the quarrymen, as they passed our cottage on their way home to the village in the valley below Moor Farm, I stepped out into the passage with a momentary notion of telling them how I was situated, and asking them for advice and protection.

I had hardly formed this idea, however, before I dismissed it. None of the quarrymen were intimate friends of mine. I had a nodding acquaintance with them, and believed them to be honest men, as times went. But my own common sense told me that what little knowledge of their characters I had was by no means sufficient to warrant me in admitting them into my confidence in the matter of the pocketbook. I had seen enough of poverty and poor men to know what a terrible temptation a large sum of money is to those whose whole lives are passed in scraping up sixpences by weary hard work. It is one thing to write fine sentiments in books about incorruptible honesty, and another thing to put those sentiments in practice, when one day's work is all that a man has to set up in the way of an obstacle between starvation and his own fireside.

The only resource that remained was to carry the pocketbook with me to Moor Farm, and ask permission to pass the night there. But I could not persuade myself that there was any real necessity for taking such a course as this; and, if the truth must be told, my pride revolted at the idea of presenting myself in the character of a coward before the people at the farm. Timidity is thought rather a graceful attraction among ladies, but among poor women it is something to be laughed at. A woman with less spirit of her own than I had, and always shall have, would have considered twice in my situation before she made up her mind to encounter the jokes of ploughmen and the jeers of milkmaids. As for me, I had hardly considered about going to the farm before I despised myself for entertaining any such notion. 'No, no,' I thought, 'I am not the woman to walk a mile and a half through rain and mist, and darkness, to tell a whole kitchenful of people that I am afraid. Come what may, here I stop till father gets back.'

Having arrived at that valiant resolution, the first thing I did was to lock and bolt the back and front doors, and see to the security of every shutter in the house.

That duty performed, I made a blazing fire, lighted my

candle, and sat down to tea, as snug and comfortable as possible. I could hardly believe now, with the light in the room, and the sense of security inspired by the closed doors and shutters, that I had ever felt even the slightest apprehension earlier in the day. I sang as I washed up the tea-things; and even the cat seemed to catch the infection of my good spirits. I never knew the pretty creature more playful than she was that evening.

The tea-things put by, I took up my knitting and worked away at it so long that I began at last to get drowsy. The fire was so bright and comforting that I could not muster resolution enough to leave it and go to bed. I sat staring lazily into the blaze, with my knitting on my lap—sat till the splashing of the rain outside, and the fitful, sullen sobbing of the wind, grew fainter and fainter on my ear. The last sounds I heard before I fairly dozed off to sleep were the cheerful crackling of the fire, and the steady purring of the cat, as she basked luxuriously in the warm light on the hearth. Those were the last sounds before I fell asleep. The sound that woke me was a loud bang at the front door.

I started up, with my heart (as the saying is) in my mouth, with a frightful momentary shuddering at the roots of my hair—I started up breathless, cold and motionless; waiting in the silence I hardly knew for what, doubtful, at first, whether I had dreamed about the bang at the door, or whether the blow had really been struck on it.

In a minute, or less, there came a second bang, louder than the first. I ran into the passage.

'Who's there?'

'Let us in,' answered a voice, which I recognized immediately as the voice of Shifty Dick.

'Wait a bit, my dear, and let me explain,' said a second voice, in the low, oily, jeering tones of Dick's companion—the wickedly clever little man whom he called Jerry. 'You are alone in the house, my pretty little dear. You may crack your sweet voice with screeching, and there's nobody near to hear you. Listen to reason, my love, and let us in. We don't want cider this time—we only want a very neat-looking pocketbook which you happen to have, and your late excellent mother's four silver teaspoons, which you keep so nice and clean on the chimney-piece. If you let us in, we won't hurt a hair of your head, my cherub, and we promise to go away the moment we have got what we want, unless you particularly wish us to stop to tea. If you keep us out, we shall be obliged to break into the house, and then—'

'And then,' burst in Shifty Dick, 'we'll *mash* you!'

'Yes,' said Jerry, 'we'll mash you, my beauty. But you won't drive us to doing that, will you? You will let us in?'

This long parley gave me time to recover from the effect which the first bang at the door had produced on my nerves. The threats of the two villains would have terrified some women out of their senses, but the only result produced on *me* was violent indignation. I had, thank God, a strong spirit of my own, and the cool, contemptuous insolence of the man Jerry effectually roused it.

'You cowardly villains!' I screamed at them through the door. 'You think you can frighten me because I am only a poor girl left alone in the house. You ragamuffin thieves, I defy you both! Our bolts are strong, our shutters are thick. I am here to keep my father's house safe, and keep it I will against an army of you!'

You may imagine what a passion I was in when I vapoured and blustered in that way. I heard Jerry laugh and Shifty Dick swear a whole mouthful of oaths. Then there was a dead silence for a minute or two; and then the two ruffians attacked the door.

I rushed into the kitchen and seized the poker, and then

heaped wood on the fire, and lighted all the candles I could find: for I felt as though I could keep up my courage better if I had plenty of light. Strange and improbable as it may appear, the next thing that attracted my attention was my poor pussy, crouched up, panic-stricken, in a corner. I was so fond of the little creature that I took her up in my arms and carried her into my bedroom and put her inside my bed. A comical thing to do in a situation of deadly peril, was it not? But it seemed quite natural and proper at the time.

All this while the blows were falling faster and faster on the door. They were dealt, as I conjectured, with heavy stones picked up from the ground outside. Jerry sang at his wicked work, and Shifty Dick swore. As I left the bedroom, after putting the cat under cover, I heard the lower panel of the door begin to crack.

I ran into the kitchen and huddled our four silver spoons into my pocket; then took the unlucky book with the banknotes and put it in the bosom of my dress. I was determined to defend the property confided to my care with my life. Just as I had secured the pocketbook I heard the door splintering, and rushed into the passage again with my heavy kitchen poker lifted in both hands.

I was in time to see the bald head of Jerry, with the ugly-looking knobs on it, pushed into the passage through a great rent in one of the lower panels of the door.

'Get out, you villain, or I'll brain you on the spot!' I screeched, threatening him with the poker.

Mr Jerry took his head out again much faster than he put it in.

The next thing that came through the rent was a long pitchfork, which they darted at me from the outside, to move me from the door. I struck at it with all my might, and the blow must have jarred the hand of Shifty Dick up to his very shoulder, for I heard him give a roar of rage and pain. Before he could catch at the fork with his other hand, I had drawn it inside. By this time, even Jerry lost his temper and swore more awfully than Dick himself.

Then there came another minute of respite. I suspected they had gone to get bigger stones, and I dreaded the giving way of the whole door.

Running into the bedroom as this fear beset me, I laid hold of my chest of drawers, dragged it into the passage, and threw it down against the door. On the top of that I heaped my father's big tool chest, three chairs, and a scuttleful of coals; and last, I dragged out the kitchen table and rammed it as hard as I could against the whole barricade. They heard me as they were coming up to the door with fresh stones. Jerry said, 'Stop a bit!' and then the two consulted together in whispers. I listened eagerly, and just caught these words:

'Let's try it the other way.'

Nothing more was said, but I heard their footsteps retreating from the door.

Were they going to besiege the back door now?

I had hardly asked myself that question when I heard their voices at the other side of the house. The back door was smaller than the front, but it had this advantage in the way of strength—it was made of two solid oak boards joined longwise, and strengthened inside by heavy cross pieces. It had no bolts like the front door, but was fastened by a bar of iron running across it in a slanting direction, and fitting at either end into the wall.

'They must have the whole cottage down before they can break in at that door!' I thought to myself. And they soon found out as much for themselves. After five minutes of banging at the back door, they gave up any farther attack in that direction, and cast their heavy stones down with curses of fury awful to hear.

I went into the kitchen and dropped on the window-seat to rest for a moment. Suspense and excitement together were beginning to tell upon me. The perspiration broke out thick on my forehead, and I began to feel the bruises I had inflicted on my hands in making the barricade against the front door. I had not lost a particle of my resolution, but I was beginning to lose strength. There was a bottle of rum in the cupboard, which my brother the sailor had left with us the last time he was ashore. I drank a drop of it. Never before or since have I put anything down my throat that did me half so much good as that precious mouthful of rum!

I was still sitting in the window-seat drying my face, when I suddenly heard their voices close behind me.

They were feeling the outside of the window against which I was sitting. It was protected, like all the other windows in the cottage, by iron bars. I listened in dreadful suspense for the sound of filing, but nothing of the sort was audible. They had evidently reckoned on frightening me easily into letting them in, and had come unprovided with house-breaking tools of any kind. A fresh burst of oaths informed me that they had recognized the obstacle of the iron bars. I listened breathlessly for some warning of what they were going to do next, but their voices seemed to die away in the distance. They were retreating from the window. Were they also retreating from the house altogether? Had they given up the idea of effecting an entrance in despair?

A long silence followed—a silence which tried my courage even more severely than the tumult of their first attack on the cottage.

Dreadful suspicions now beset me of their being able to accomplish by treachery what they had failed to effect by force. Well as I knew the cottage, I began to doubt whether there might not be ways of cunningly and silently entering it against which I was not provided. The ticking of the clock annoyed me; the crackling of the fire startled me. I looked out twenty times in a minute into the dark corners of the passage, straining my eyes, holding my breath, anticipating the most unlikely events, the most impossible dangers. Had they really gone? or were they still prowling about the house? Oh, what a sum of money I would have given only to have known what they were about in that interval of silence!

I was startled at last out of my suspense in the most awful manner. A shout from one of them reached my ears on a sudden down the kitchen chimney. It was so unexpected and so horrible in the stillness that I screamed for the first time since the attack on the house. My worst forebodings had never suggested to me that the two villains might mount upon the roof.

'Let us in, you she-devil!' roared a voice down the chimney.

There was another pause. The smoke from the wood fire, thin and light as it was in the red state of the embers at that moment, had evidently obliged the man to take his face from the mouth of the chimney. I counted the seconds while he was, as I conjectured, getting his breath again. In less than half a minute there came another shout:

'Let us in, or we'll burn the place down over your head.'

Burn it? Burn what? There was nothing easily combustible but the thatch on the roof; and that had been well soaked by the heavy rain which had now fallen incessantly for more than six hours. Burn the place over my head? How?

While I was still casting about wildly in my mind to discover what possible danger there could be of fire, one of the heavy stones, placed on the thatch to keep it from being torn up by high winds, came thundering down the chimney. It scattered the live embers on the hearth all over the room. A richly furnished place, with knick-knacks and fine muslin about it, would have been set on fire immediately. Even our bare floor and rough furniture gave out a smell of burning at the first shower of embers which the first stone scattered.

For an instant I stood quite horror-struck before this new proof of the devilish ingenuity of the villains outside. But the dreadful danger I was now in recalled me to my senses immediately. There was a large canful of water in my bedroom, and I ran in at once to fetch it. Before I could get back to the kitchen, a second stone had been thrown down the chimney, and the floor was smouldering in several places.

I had wit enough to let the smouldering go on for a moment or two more, and to pour the whole of my canful of water over the fire before the third stone came down the chimney. The live embers on the floor I easily disposed of after that. The man on the roof must have heard the hissing of the fire as I put it out, and have felt the change produced in the air at the mouth of the chimney; for after the third stone had descended, no more followed it. As for either of the ruffians themselves dropping down by the same road along which the stones had come, that was not to be dreaded. The chimney, as I well knew by our experience in cleaning it, was too narrow to give passage to any one above the size of a small boy.

I looked upwards as that comforting reflection crossed my mind—I looked up, and saw, as plainly as I see the paper I am now writing on, the point of a knife coming through the inside of the roof, just over my head. Our cottage had no upper storey, and our rooms had no ceilings. Slowly and wickedly the knife wriggled its way through the dry inside thatch between the rafters. It stopped for a while, and there came a sound of tearing. That, in its turn, stopped too; there was a great fall of dry thatch on the floor; and I saw the heavy, hairy hand of Shifty Dick, armed with the knife, come through after the fallen fragments. He tapped at the rafters with the back of the knife, as if to test their strength. Thank God, they were substantial and close together! Nothing lighter than a hatchet would have sufficed to remove any part of them.

The murderous hand was still tapping with the knife, when I heard a shout from the man Jerry, coming from the neighbourhood of my father's stone-shed in the back yard. The hand and knife disappeared instantly. I went to the back door, and put my ear to it and listened.

Both men were now in the shed. I made the most desperate efforts to call to mind what tools and other things were left in it, which might be used against me. But my agitation confused me. I could remember nothing except my father's big stone-saw, which was far too heavy and unwieldy to be used on the roof of the cottage. I was still puzzling my brains and making my head swim to no purpose, when I heard the men dragging something out of the shed. At the same instant when the noise caught my ear, the remembrance flashed across me like lightning of some beams of wood which had lain in the shed for years past. I had hardly time to feel certain that they were removing one of these beams before I heard Shifty Dick say to Jerry:

'Which door?'

'The front,' was the answer. 'We've cracked it already; we'll have it down now in no time.'

Senses less sharpened by danger than mine would have understood but too easily, from these words, that they were about to use the beam as a battering-ram against the door. When that conviction overcame me, I lost courage at last. I felt that the door must come down. No such barricade as I had constructed could support it, for more than a few minutes, against such shocks as it was now to receive.

'I can do no more to keep the house against them,' I said to myself, with my knees knocking together, and the tears at last beginning to wet my cheeks. 'I must trust to the night and the thick darkness, and save my life by running for it, while there is yet time.'

I huddled on my cloak and hood, and had my hand on the bar of the back door, when a piteous mew from the bedroom reminded me of the existence of poor pussy. I ran in, and huddled the creature up in my apron. Before I was out in the passage again, the first shock from the beam fell on the door.

The upper hinge gave way. The chairs and the coal-skuttle forming the top of my barricade were hurled, rattling, on to the floor, but the lower hinge of the door, and the chest of drawers and tool-chest, still kept their places.

'One more,' I heard the villains cry—'one more run with the beam, and down it comes!'

Just as they must have been starting for that 'one more run', I opened the back door and fled out into the night, with the bookful of banknotes in my bosom, the silver spoons in my pocket, and the cat in my arms. I threaded my way easily enough through the familiar obstacles in the backyard, and was out in the pitch darkness of the moor before I heard the second shock, and the crash which told me that the whole door had given way.

In a few minutes they must have discovered the fact of my flight with the pocketbook, for I heard shouts in the distance as if they were running out to pursue me. I kept on at the top of my speed, and the noise soon died away. It was so dark that twenty thieves, instead of two, would have found it useless to follow me.

How long it was before I reached the farmhouse—the nearest place to which I could fly for refuge—I cannot tell you. I remember that I had just sense enough to keep the wind at my back (having observed in the beginning of the evening that it blew toward Moor Farm), and to go on resolutely through the darkness. In all other respects, I was by this time half crazed by what I had gone through. If it had so happened that the wind had changed after I had observed its direction early in the evening, I should have gone astray, and have probably perished of fatigue and exposure on the moor. Providentially, it still blew steadily, as it had blown for hours past, and I reached the farmhouse with my clothes wet through, and my brain in a high fever. When I made my alarm at the door, they had all gone to bed but the farmer's eldest son, who was sitting up late over his pipe and newspaper. I just mustered strength enough to gasp out a few words, telling him what was the matter, and then fell down at his feet, for the first time in my life in a dead swoon.

That swoon was followed by a severe illness. When I got strong enough to look about me again, I found myself in one of the farmhouse beds—my father, Mrs Knifton, and the doctor were all in the room—my cat was asleep at my feet, and the pocketbook that I had saved lay on the table by my side.

There was plenty of news for me to hear, as soon as I was fit to listen to it. Shifty Dick and the other rascal had been caught, and were in prison, waiting their trial at the next assizes. Mr and Mrs Knifton had been so shocked at the danger I had run—for which they blamed their own want of thoughtfulness in leaving the pocketbook in my care—that they had insisted on my father's removing from our lonely home to a cottage on their land, which we were to inhabit rent free. The banknotes that I had saved were given to me to buy furniture with, in place of the things that the thieves had broken. These pleasant tidings assisted so greatly in promoting my recovery that I was soon able to relate to my friends at the farmhouse the particulars that I have written here. They were all surprised and interested, but no one, as I thought, listened to me with such breathless attention as the farmer's eldest son. Mrs Knifton noticed this, too, and began to make jokes about it, in her light-hearted way, as soon as we were alone. I thought little of her jesting at the time; but when I got well, and we went to live at our new home, 'the young farmer', as he was called in our parts, constantly came to see us, and constantly managed to meet me out of doors. I had my share of vanity, like other young women, and I began to think of Mrs Knifton's jokes with some attention. To be brief, the young farmer managed one Sunday—I never could tell how—to lose his way with me in returning from church, and before we found out the right road home again, he had asked me to be his wife.

His relations did all they could to keep us asunder and break off the match, thinking a poor stonemason's daughter no fit wife for a prosperous yeoman. But the farmer was too obstinate for them. He had one form of answer to all their objections. 'A man, if he is worth the name, marries according to his own notions, and to please himself,' he used to say. 'My notion is that when I take a wife I am placing my character and my happiness—the most precious things I have to trust—in one woman's care. The woman I mean to marry had a small charge confided to her care, and showed herself worthy of it at the risk of her life. That is proof enough for me that she is worthy of the greatest charge I can put into her hands. Rank and riches are fine things, but the certainty of getting a good wife is something better still. I'm of age, I know my own mind, and I mean to marry the stonemason's daughter.'

And he did marry me. Whether I proved myself worthy or not of his good opinion is a question which I must leave you to ask my husband. All that I had to relate about myself and my doings is now told. Whatever interest my perilous adventure may excite ends, I am well aware, with my escape to the farmhouse. I have only ventured on writing these few additional sentences because my marriage is the moral of my story. It has brought me the choicest blessings of happiness and prosperity, and I owe them all to my night adventure in the Black Cottage.

2

BROTHER GRIFFITH'S STORY OF THE FAMILY SECRET

Chapter I

Was it an Englishman or a Frenchman who first remarked that every family had a skeleton in its cupboard? I am not learned enough to know, but I reverence the observation, whoever made it. It speaks a startling truth through an appropriately grim metaphor—a truth which I have discovered by practical experience. Our family had a skeleton in the cupboard, and the name of it was Uncle George.

I arrived at the knowledge that this skeleton existed, and I traced it to the particular cupboard in which it was hidden, by slow degrees. I was a child when I first began to suspect that there was such a thing, and a grown man when I at last discovered that my suspicions were true.

My father was a doctor, having an excellent practice in a large country town. I have heard that he married against the wishes of his family. They could not object to my mother on the score of birth, breeding, or character—they only disliked her heartily. My grandfather, grandmother, uncles and aunts, all declared that she was a heartless, deceitful woman; all disliked her manners, her opinions, and even the expression of her face—all, with the exception of my father's youngest brother, George.

George was the unlucky member of our family. The rest were all clever; he was slow in capacity. The rest were all remarkably handsome; he was the sort of man that no woman ever looks at twice. The rest succeeded in life; he failed. His profession was the same as my father's, but he never got on when he started in practice for himself. The sick poor, who could not choose, employed him, and liked him. The sick rich, who could—especially the ladies—declined to call him in when they could get anybody else. In experience he gained greatly by his profession; in money and reputation he gained nothing.

There are very few of us, however dull and unattractive we may be to outward appearance, who have not some strong passion, some germ of what is called romance, hidden more or less deeply in our natures. All the passion and romance in the nature of my Uncle George lay in his love and admiration for my father.

He sincerely worshipped his eldest brother as one of the noblest of human beings. When my father was engaged to be married, and when the rest of the family, as I have already mentioned, did not hesitate to express their unfavourable opinion of the disposition of his chosen wife, Uncle George, who had never ventured on differing with anyone before, to the amazement of everybody, undertook the defence of his future sister-in-law in the most vehement and positive manner. In his estimation, his brother's choice was something sacred and indisputable. The lady might, and did, treat him with unconcealed contempt, laugh at his awkwardness, grow impatient at his stammering—it made no difference to Uncle George. It was enough for him that she was to be his brother's wife, and, in virtue of that one great fact, she became, in the estimation of the poor surgeon, a very queen, who, by the laws of the domestic constitution, could do no wrong.

When my father had been married a little while, he took his youngest brother to live with him as his assistant. If Uncle George had been made president of the College of Surgeons, he could not have been prouder and happier than he was in his new position. I am afraid my father never understood the depth of his brother's affection for him. All the hard work fell to George's share: the long journeys at night, the physicking of wearisome poor people, the drunken cases, the revolting cases—all the drudging, dirty business of the surgery, in short, was turned over to him; and day after day, month after month, he struggled through it without a murmur. When his brother and his sister-in-law went out to dine with the county gentry, it never entered his head to feel disappointed at being left unnoticed at home. When the return dinners were given, and he was asked to come in at teatime and left to sit unregarded in a corner, it never occurred to him to imagine that he was treated with any want of consideration or respect. He was part of the furniture of the house, and it was the business as well as the pleasure of his life to turn himself to any use to which his brother might please to put him.

So much for what I have heard from others on the subject of my Uncle George. My own personal experience of him is limited to what I remember as a mere child. Let me say something however, first about my parents, my sister and myself.

My sister was the eldest born, and the best loved. I did not come into the world till four years after her birth, and no other child followed me. Caroline, from her earliest days, was the perfection of beauty and health. I was small, weakly, and, if the truth must be told, almost as plain-featured as Uncle George himself. It would be ungracious and undutiful in me to presume to decide whether there was any foundation or not for the dislike that my father's family always felt for my mother. All I can venture to say is that her children never had any cause to complain of her.

Her passionate affection for my sister, her pride in the child's beauty, I remember well, as also her uniform kindness and indulgence towards me. My personal defects must have been a sore trial to her in secret, but neither she nor my father ever showed me that they perceived any difference between Caroline and myself. When presents were made to my sister, presents were made to me. When my father and mother caught my sister up in their arms and kissed her, they scrupulously gave me my turn afterwards. My childish instinct told me that there was a difference in their smiles when they looked at me and looked at her; that the kisses given to Caroline were warmer than the kisses given to me; that the hands which dried her tears in our childish griefs touched her more gently than the hands which dried mine. But these, and other small signs of preference like them, were such as no parents could be expected to control. I noticed them at the time rather with wonder than with repining. I recall them now, without a harsh thought, either towards my father or my mother. Both loved me, and both did their duty by me. If I seem to speak constrainedly of them here, it is not on my own account. I can honestly say that, with all my heart and soul.

Even Uncle George, fond as he was of me, was fonder of my beautiful child-sister. When I used mischievously to pull at his lank, scanty hair, he would gently and laughingly take it out of my hands, but he would let Caroline tug at it till his dim, wandering grey eyes winked and watered again with pain. He used to plunge perilously about the garden, in awkward imitation of the cantering of a horse, while I sat on his shoulders; but he would never proceed at any pace beyond a slow and safe walk when Caroline had a ride in her turn. When he took us out walking, Caroline was always on the side next the wall. When we interrupted him over his dirty work in the surgery, he used to tell me to go and play until he was ready for me; but he would put down his bottles, and clean his clumsy fingers on his coarse apron, and lead Caroline out again, as if she had been the greatest lady in the land. Ah, how he loved her!—and, let me be honest and grateful, and add, how he loved me too!

When I was eight years old and Caroline was twelve, I was separated from home for some time. I had been ailing for many months previously; had got benefit from being taken to the seaside, and had shown symptoms of relapsing on being brought home again to the midland county in which we resided. After much consultation, it was at last resolved that I should be sent to live, until my constitution got stronger, with a maiden sister of my mother's, who had a house at a watering-place on the south coast.

I left home, I remember, loaded with presents, rejoicing over the prospect of looking at the sea again, as careless of the future and as happy in the present as any boy could be. Uncle George petitioned for a holiday to take me to the seaside, but he could not be spared from the surgery. He consoled himself and me by promising to make me a magnificent model of a ship.

I have that model before my eyes now, while I write. It is dusty with age; the paint on it is cracked; the ropes are tangled; the sails are moth-eaten and yellow. The hull is all out of proportion, and the rig has been smiled at by every nautical friend of mine who has ever looked at it. Yet, worn-out and faulty as it is—inferior to the cheapest miniature vessel nowadays in any toyshop window—I hardly know a possession of mine in this world that I would not sooner part with than Uncle George's ship.

My life at the seaside was a very happy one. I remained with my aunt more than a year. My mother often came to see how I was going on; and, at first, always brought my sister with her; but, during the last eight months of my stay, Caroline never once appeared. I noticed also, at the same period, a change in my mother's manner. She looked paler and more anxious at each succeeding visit, and always had long conferences in private with my aunt. At last she ceased to come and see us altogether, and only wrote to know how my health was getting on. My father, too, who had at the earlier periods of my absence from home travelled to the seaside to watch the progress of my recovery, as often as his professional engagements would permit, now kept away like my mother. Even Uncle George, who had never been allowed a holiday to come and see me, but who had hitherto often written, and begged me to write to him, broke off our correspondence.

I was naturally perplexed and amazed by these changes, and persecuted my aunt to tell me the reason of them. At first she tried to put me off with excuses; then she admitted that there was trouble in our house; and finally she confessed that the trouble was caused by the illness of my sister. When I enquired what that illness was, my aunt said it was useless to attempt to explain it to me. I next applied to the servants. One of them was less cautious than my aunt, and answered my question, but in terms that I could not comprehend. After much explanation, I was made to understand that 'something was growing on my sister's neck that would spoil her beauty forever, and perhaps kill her, if it could not be got rid of'.

How well I remember the shudder of horror that ran through me at the vague idea of this deadly 'something'! A fearful, awestruck curiosity to see what Caroline's illness was with my own eyes troubled my inmost heart, and I begged to be allowed to go home and help to nurse her. The request was, it is almost needless to say, refused.

Weeks passed away, and still I heard nothing, except that my sister continued to be ill. One day I privately wrote a letter to Uncle George, asking him, in my childish way, to come and tell me about Caroline's illness.

I knew where the post-office was, and slipped out in the morning, unobserved, and dropped my letter in the box. I stole home again by the garden, and climbed in at the window of a back parlour on the ground floor. The room above was my aunt's bedchamber, and the moment I was inside the house I heard moans and loud convulsive sobs proceeding from it. My aunt was a singularly quiet, composed woman. I could not imagine that the loud sobbing and moaning came from her, and I ran down terrified into the kitchen to ask the servants who was crying so violently in my aunt's room.

I found the housemaid and the cook talking together in whispers, with serious faces. They started when they saw me, as if I had been a grown-up master who had caught them neglecting their work.

'He's too young to feel it much,' I heard one say to the other. 'So far as he is concerned, it seems like a mercy that it happened no later.'

In a few minutes they had told me the worst. It was my aunt who had been crying in the bedroom. Caroline was dead.

I felt the blow more severely than the servants or anyone else about me supposed. Still, I was a child in years, and I had the blessed elasticity of a child's nature. If I had been older, I might have been too much absorbed in grief to observe my aunt so closely as I did, when she was composed enough to see me, later in the day.

I was not surprised by the swollen state of her eyes, the paleness of her cheeks, or the fresh burst of tears that came from her when she took me in her arms at meeting. But I was both amazed and perplexed by the look of terror that I detected in her face. It was natural enough that she should grieve and weep over my sister's death; but why should she have that frightened look, as if some other catastrophe had happened?

I asked if there was any more dreadful news from home besides the news of Caroline's death? My aunt said, 'No,' in a strange, stifled voice, and suddenly turned her face from me. Was my father dead? No. My mother? No. Uncle George? My aunt trembled all over as she said No to that also, and bade me cease asking any more questions. She was not fit to bear them yet, she said, and signed to the servant to lead me out of the room.

The next day I was told that I was to go home after the funeral, and was taken out towards evening by the housemaid, partly for a walk, partly to be measured for my mourning clothes. After we had left the tailor's, I persuaded the girl to extend our walk for some distance along the sea-beach, telling her, as we went, every little anecdote connected with my lost sister that came tenderly back to my memory in those first days of sorrow. She was so interested in hearing, and I in speaking, that we let the sun go down before we thought of turning back.

The evening was cloudy, and it got on from dusk to dark by the time we approached the town again. The housemaid was rather nervous at finding herself alone with me on the beach, and once or twice looked behind her distrustfully as we went on. Suddenly she squeezed my hand hard, and said:

'Let's get up on the cliff as fast as we can.'

The words were hardly out of her mouth before I heard footsteps behind me—a man came round quickly to my side, snatched me away from the girl, and, catching me up in his arms, without a word, covered my face with kisses. I knew he was crying, because my cheeks were instantly wet with his tears; but it was too dark for me to see who he was, or even how he was dressed. He did not, I should think, hold me half a minute in his arms. The housemaid screamed for help. I was put down gently on the sand, and the strange man instantly disappeared in the darkness.

When this extraordinary adventure was related to my aunt, she seemed at first merely bewildered at hearing of it; but in a moment more there came a change over her face, as if she had suddenly recollected or thought of something. She turned deadly pale, and said, in a hurried way, very unusual with her:

'Never mind; don't talk about it any more. It was only a mischievous trick to frighten you, I dare say. Forget all about it, my dear—forget all about it.'

It was easier to give this advice than to make me follow it. For many nights after, I thought of nothing but the strange man who had kissed me and cried over me. Who could he be? Somebody who loved me very much, and who was very sorry. My childish logic carried me to that length. But when I tried to think over all the grown-up gentlemen who loved me very much, I could never get on, to my own satisfaction, beyond my father and my Uncle George.

Chapter II

I was taken home on the appointed day to suffer the trial—a hard one even at my tender years—of witnessing my mother's passionate grief and my father's mute despair. I remember that the scene of our first meeting after Caroline's death was wisely and considerately shortened by my aunt, who took me out of the room. She seemed to have a confused desire to keep me from leaving her after the door had closed behind us; but I broke away and ran downstairs to the surgery, to go and cry for my lost playmate with the sharer of all our games, Uncle George.

I opened the surgery door, and could see nobody. I dried my tears and looked all round the room—it was empty. I ran upstairs again to Uncle George's garret bedroom—he was not there; his cheap hairbrush and old cast-off razor-case, that had belonged to my grandfather, were not on the dressing-table. Had he got some other bedroom? I went out on the landing, and called softly, with an unaccountable terror and sinking at my heart:

'Uncle George!'

Nobody answered; but my aunt came hastily up the garret stairs.

'Hush!' she said. 'You must never mention that name here again!'

She stopped suddenly, and looked as if her own words had frightened her.

'Is Uncle George dead?' I asked. My aunt turned red and pale, and stammered.

I did not wait to hear what she said. I brushed past her, down the stairs.—My heart was bursting—my flesh felt cold. I ran breathlessly and recklessly into the room where my father and mother had received me. They were both sitting there still. I ran up to them, wringing my hands, and crying out in a passion of tears:

'Is Uncle George dead?'

My mother gave a scream that terrified me into instant silence and stillness. My father looked at her for a moment, rang the bell that summoned the maid, then seized me roughly by the arm and dragged me out of the room.

He took me down into the study, seated himself in his accustomed chair, and put me before him between his knees. His lips were awfully white, and I felt his two hands, as they grasped my shoulders, shaking violently.

'You are never to mention the name of Uncle George

again,' he said, in a quick, angry, trembling whisper. 'Never to me, never to your mother, never to your aunt, never to anybody in this world! Never—never—never!'

The repetition of the word terrified me even more than the suppressed vehemence with which he spoke. He saw that I was frightened, and softened his manner a little before he went on.

'You will never see Uncle George again,' he said. 'Your mother and I love you dearly; but if you forget what I have told you, you will be sent away from home. Never speak that name again—mind, never! Now kiss me, and go away.'

How his lips trembled—and, oh, how cold they felt on mine!

I shrank out of the room the moment he had kissed me, and went and hid myself in the garden.

'Uncle George is gone. I am never to see him any more, I am never to speak of him again—those were the words I repeated to myself, with indescribable terror and confusion, the moment I was alone. There was something unspeakably horrible to my young mind in this mystery which I was commanded always to respect, and which, so far as I then knew, I could never hope to see revealed. My father, my mother, my aunt, all appeared to be separated from me now by some impassable barrier. Home seemed home no longer with Caroline dead, Uncle George gone, and a forbidden subject of talk perpetually and mysteriously interposing between my parents and me.

Though I never infringed the command my father had given me in his study (his words and looks, and that dreadful scream of my mother's, which seemed to be still ringing in my ears, were more than enough to ensure my obedience), I also never lost the secret desire to penetrate the darkness which clouded over the fate of Uncle George.

For two years I remained at home and discovered nothing. If I asked the servants about my uncle, they could only tell me that one morning he disappeared from the house. Of the members of my father's family I could make no inquiries. They lived far away, and never came to see us; and the idea of writing to them, at my age and in my position, was out of the question. My aunt was as unapproachably silent as my father and mother; but I never forgot how her face had altered when she reflected for a moment after hearing of my extraordinary adventure while going home with the servant over the sands at night. The more I thought of that change of countenance in connection with what had occurred on my return to my father's house, the more certain I felt that the stranger who had kissed me and wept over me must have been no other than Uncle George.

At the end of my two years at home I was sent to sea in the merchant navy by my own earnest desire. I had always determined to be a sailor from the time when I first went to stay with my aunt at the seaside,— and I persisted long enough in my resolution to make my parents recognize the necessity of acceding to my wishes.

My new life delighted me, and I remained away on foreign stations more than four years. When I at length returned home, it was to find a new affliction darkening our fireside. My father had died on the very day when I sailed for my return voyage to England.

Absence and change of scene had in no respect weakened my desire to penetrate the mystery of Uncle George's disappearance. My mother's health was so delicate that I hesitated for some time to approach the forbidden subject in her presence. When I at last ventured to refer to it, suggesting to her that any prudent reserve which might have been necessary while I was a child, need no longer be persisted in, now that I was growing to be a young man, she fell into a violent fit of trembling, and commanded me to say no more. It had been my father's will, she said, that the reserve to which I referred should be always adopted towards me; he had not authorized her, before he died, to speak more openly; and, now that he was gone, she would not so much as think of acting on her own unaided judgment. My aunt said the same thing in effect when I appealed to her. Determined not to be discouraged even yet, I undertook a journey, ostensibly to pay my respects to my father's family, but with the secret intention of trying what I could learn in that quarter on the subject of Uncle George.

My investigations led to some results, though they were by no means satisfactory. George had always been looked upon with something like contempt by his handsome sisters and his prosperous brothers, and he had not improved his position in the family by his warm advocacy of his brother's cause at the time of my father's marriage. I found that my uncle's surviving relatives now spoke of him slightingly and carelessly. They assured me that they had never heard from him, and that they knew nothing about him, except that he had gone away to settle, as they supposed, in some foreign place, after having behaved very basely and badly to my father. He had been traced to London, where he had sold out of the funds the small share of money which he had inherited after his father's death, and he had been seen on the deck of a packet bound for France later on the same day. Beyond this nothing was known about him. In what the alleged baseness of his behaviour had consisted none of his brothers and sisters could tell me. My father had refused to pain them by going into particulars, not only at the time of his brother's disappearance, but afterwards, whenever the subject was mentioned. George had always been the black sheep of the flock, and he must have been conscious of his own baseness, or he would certainly have written to explain and to justify himself.

Such were the particulars which I gleaned during my

visit to my father's family. To my mind, they tended rather to deepen than to reveal the mystery. That such a gentle, docile, affectionate creature as Uncle George should have injured the brother he loved, by word or deed at any period of their intercourse, seemed incredible; but that he should have been guilty of an act of baseness at the very time when my sister was dying was simply and plainly impossible. And yet there was the incomprehensible fact staring me in the face that the death of Caroline and the disappearance of Uncle George had taken place in the same week! Never did I feel more daunted and bewildered by the family secret than after I had heard all the particulars in connection with it that my father's relatives had to tell me.

I may pass over the events of the next few years of my life briefly enough.

My nautical pursuits filled up all my time, and took me far away from my country and my friends. But, whatever I did, and wherever I went, the memory of Uncle George, and the desire to penetrate the mystery of his disappearance, haunted me like familiar spirits. Often, in the lonely watches of the night at sea, did I recall the dark evening on the beach, the strange man's hurried embrace, the startling sensation of feeling his tears on my cheeks, the disappearance of him before I had breath or self-possession enough to say a word. Often did I think over the inexplicable events that followed, when I had returned, after my sister's funeral, to my father's house; and oftener still did I puzzle my brains vainly, in the attempt to form some plan for inducing my mother or my aunt to disclose the secret which they had hitherto kept from me so perseveringly. My only chance of knowing what had really happened to Uncle George, my only hope of seeing him again, rested with those two near and dear relatives. I despaired of ever getting my mother to speak on the forbidden subject after what had passed between us, but I felt more sanguine about my prospects of ultimately inducing my aunt to relax in her discretion. My anticipations, however, in this direction were not destined to be fulfilled. On my next visit to England I found my aunt prostrated by a paralytic attack, which deprived her of the power of speech. She died soon afterwards in my arms, leaving me her sole heir. I searched anxiously among her papers for some reference to the family mystery, but found no clue to guide me. All my mother's letters to her sister at the time of Caroline's illness and death had been destroyed.

Chapter III

More years passed; my mother followed my aunt to the grave, and still I was as far as ever from making any discoveries in relation to Uncle George. Shortly after the period of this last affliction my health gave way, and I departed, by my doctor's advice, to try some baths in the South of France.

I travelled slowly to my destination, turning aside from the direct road, and stopping wherever I pleased. One evening, when I was not more than two or three days' journey from the baths to which I was bound, I was struck by the picturesque situation of a little town placed on the brow of a hill at some distance from the main road, and resolved to have a nearer look at the place, with a view to stopping there for the night, if it pleased me. I found the principal inn clean and quiet—ordered my bed there—and, after dinner, strolled out to look at the church. No thought of Uncle George was in my mind when I entered the building; and yet, at that very moment, chance was leading me to the discovery which, for so many years past, I had vainly endeavoured to make—the discovery which I had given up as hopeless since the day of my mother's death.

I found nothing worth notice in the church, and was about

to leave it again, when I caught a glimpse of a pretty view through a side door, and stopped to admire it.

The churchyard formed the foreground, and below it the hillside sloped away gently into the plain, over which the sun was setting in full glory. The curé of the church was reading his breviary, walking up and down a gravel path that parted the rows of graves. In the course of my wanderings I had learnt to speak French as fluently as most Englishmen; and when the priest came near me I said a few words in praise of the view, and complimented him on the neatness and prettiness of the churchyard. He answered with great politeness, and we got into conversation together immediately.

As we strolled along the gravel walk, my attention was attracted by one of the graves standing apart from the rest. The cross at the head of it differed remarkably, in some points of appearance, from the crosses on the other graves. While all the rest had garlands hung on them, this one cross was quite bare; and, more extraordinary still, no name was inscribed on it.

The priest, observing that I stopped to look at the grave, shook his head and sighed.

'A countryman of yours is buried there,' he said, 'I was present at his death. He had borne the burden of a great sorrow among us, in this town, for many weary years, and his conduct had taught us to respect and pity him with all our hearts.'

'How is it that his name is not inscribed over his grave?' I inquired.

'It was suppressed by his own desire,' answered the priest, with some little hesitation. 'He acknowledged to me in his last moments that he had lived here under an assumed name. I asked his real name, and he told it to me, with the particulars of his sad story. He had reason for desiring to be forgotten after his death. Almost the last words he spoke were, "Let my name die with me!" Almost the last request he made was that

I would keep that name a secret from all the world excepting only one person.'

'Some relative, I suppose?' said I.

'Yes—a nephew,' said the priest.

The moment the last word was out of his mouth, my heart gave a strange answering bound. I suppose I must have changed colour also, for the curé looked at me with sudden attention and interest.

'A nephew,' the priest went on, 'whom he had loved like his own child. He told me that if this nephew ever traced him to his burial place, and asked about him, I was free in that case to disclose all I knew. "I should like my little Charley to know the truth," he said. "In spite of the difference in our ages, Charley and I were playmates years ago."'

My heart beat faster, and I felt a choking sensation at the throat the moment I heard the priest unconsciously mention my Christian name in reporting the dying man's last words.

As soon as I could steady my voice and feel certain of my self-possession, I communicated my family name to the curé, and asked him if that was not part of the secret that he had been requested to preserve.

He started back several steps, and clasped his hands amazedly.

'Can it be?' he said, in low tones, gazing at me earnestly, with something like dread in his face.

I gave him my passport, and looked away towards the grave. The tears came into my eyes as the recollections of past days crowded back on me. Hardly knowing what I did, I knelt down by the grave, and smoothed the grass over it with my hand. Oh, Uncle George, why not have told your secret to your old playmate? Why leave him to find you *here*?

The priest raised me gently, and begged me to go with him into his own house. On our way there, I mentioned persons and places that I thought my uncle might have spoken of, in order to satisfy my companion that I was really the person I represented myself to be. By the time we had entered his little parlour, and had sat down alone in it, we were almost like old friends together.

I thought it best that I should begin by telling all that I have related here on the subject of Uncle George, and his disappearance from home. My host listened with a very sad face, and said, when I had done:

'I can understand your anxiety to know what I am authorized to tell you, but pardon me if I say first that there are circumstances in your uncle's story which it may pain you to hear—' He stopped suddenly.

'Which it may pain me to hear as a nephew?' I asked.

'No,' said the priest, looking away from me, 'as a son.'

I gratefully expressed my sense of the delicacy and kindness which had prompted my companion's warning, but I begged him, at the same time, to keep me no longer in suspense and to tell me the stern truth, no matter how painfully it might affect me as a listener.

'In telling me all you know about what you term the Family Secret,' said the priest, 'you have mentioned as a strange coincidence that your sister's death and your uncle's disappearance took place at the same time. Did you ever suspect what cause it was that occasioned your sister's death?'

'I only knew what my father told me, and what all our friends believed—that she died of a tumour in the neck, or, as I sometimes heard it stated, from the effect on her constitution of a tumour in the neck.'

'She died under an operation for the removal of that tumour,' said the priest, in low tones; 'and the operator was your Uncle George.'

In those few words all the truth burst upon me.

'Console yourself with the thought that the long martyrdom of his life is over,' the priest went on. 'He rests: he is at peace. He and his little darling understand each other, and are happy now. That thought bore him up to the last, on his deathbed. He always spoke of your sister as his "little darling." He firmly believed that she was waiting to forgive and console him in the other world—and who shall say he was deceived in that belief?'

Not I! Not anyone who has ever loved and suffered, surely!

'It was out of the depth of his self-sacrificing love for the child that he drew the fatal courage to undertake the operation,' continued the priest. 'Your father naturally shrank from attempting it. His medical brethren whom he consulted all doubted the propriety of taking any measures for the removal of the tumour, in the particular condition and situation of it when they were called in. Your uncle alone differed with them. He was too modest a man to say so, but your mother found it out. The deformity of her beautiful child horrified her. She was desperate enough to catch at the faintest hope of remedying it that anyone might hold out to her; and she persuaded your uncle to put his opinion to the proof. Her horror at the deformity of the child, and her despair at the prospect of its lasting for life, seem to have utterly blinded her to all natural sense of the danger of the operation. It is hard to know how to say it to you, her son, but it must be told, nevertheless, that one day, when your father was out, she untruly informed your uncle that his brother had consented to the performance of the operation, and that he had gone purposely out of the house because he had not nerve enough to stay and witness it. After that, your uncle no longer hesitated. He had no fear of results, provided he could be certain of his own courage. All he dreaded was the effect on him of his love for the child when he first found himself face to face with the dreadful necessity of touching her skin with the knife.'

I tried hard to control myself, but I could not repress a shudder at those words.

'It is useless to shock you by going into particulars,' said the priest, considerately. 'Let it be enough if I say that your uncle's fortitude failed to support him when he wanted it most. His love for the child shook the firm hand which had never trembled before. In a word, the operation failed. Your father returned, and found his child dying. The frenzy of his despair when the truth was told him carried him to excesses which it shocks me to mention—excesses which began in his degrading his brother by a blow, which ended in his binding himself by an oath to make that brother suffer public punishment for his fatal rashness in a court of law. Your uncle was too heartbroken by what had happened to feel those outrages as some men might have felt them. He looked for one moment at his sister-in-law (I do not like to say your mother, considering what I have now to tell you), to see if she would acknowledge that she had encouraged him to attempt the operation, and that she had deceived him in saying that he had his brother's permission to try it. She was silent, and when she spoke, it was to join her husband in denouncing him as the murderer of their child. Whether fear of your father's anger, or revengeful indignation against your uncle most actuated her, I cannot presume to inquire in your presence. I can only state facts.'

The priest paused and looked at me anxiously. I could not speak to him at that moment—I could only encourage him to proceed by pressing his hand.

He resumed in these terms:

'Meanwhile, your uncle turned to your father, and spoke the last words he was ever to address to his eldest brother in this world. He said, "I have deserved the worst your anger can inflict on me, but I will spare you the scandal of bringing me to justice in open court. The law, if it found me guilty, could at the worst but banish me from my country and my friends. I will go of my own accord. God is my witness that I honestly believed I could save the child from deformity and suffering. I have risked all and lost all. My heart and spirit are broken. I am fit for nothing, but to go and hide myself, and my shame and misery, from all eyes that have ever looked on me. I shall never come back, never expect your pity or forgiveness. If you think less harshly of me when I am gone, keep secret what has happened; let no other lips say of me what yours and your wife's have said. I shall think that forbearance atonement enough—atonement greater than I have deserved. Forget me in this world. May we meet in another, where the secrets of all hearts are opened, and where the child who is gone before may make peace between us!" He said those words and went out. Your father never saw him or heard from him again.'

I knew the reason now why my father had never confided the truth to anyone, his own family included. My mother had evidently confessed all to her sister under the seal of secrecy, and there the dreadful disclosure had been arrested.

'Your uncle told me,' the priest continued, 'that before he left England he took leave of you by stealth, in a place you were staying at by the seaside. He had not the heart to quit his country and his friends forever without kissing you for the last time. He followed you in the dark, and caught you up in his arms, and left you again before you had a chance of discovering him. The next day he quitted England.'

'For this place?' I asked.

'Yes. He had spent a week here once with a student friend at the time when he was a pupil in the Hotel Dieu, and to this place he returned to hide, to suffer, and to die. We all saw that he was a man crushed and broken by some great sorrow, and we respected him and his affliction. He lived alone, and only came out of doors towards evening, when he used to sit on the brow of the hill yonder, with his head on his hand, looking towards England. That place seemed a favourite with him, and he is buried close by it. He revealed the story of his past life to no living soul here but me; and to me he only spoke when his last hour was approaching. What he had suffered during his long exile no man can presume to say. I, who saw more of him than anyone, never heard a word of complaint fall from his lips. He had the courage of the martyrs while he lived, and the resignation of the saints when he died. Just at the last his mind wandered. He said he saw his little darling waiting by the bedside to lead him away; and he died with a smile on his face—the first I had ever seen there.'

The priest ceased, and we went out together in the mournful twilight, and stood for a little while on the brow of the hill where Uncle George used to sit, with his face turned towards England. How my heart ached for him as I thought of what he must have suffered in the silence and solitude of his long exile! Was it well for me that I had discovered the Family Secret at last? I have sometimes thought not. I have sometimes wished that the darkness had never been cleared away which once hid from me the fate of Uncle George.

3

FARMER FAIRWEATHER

I am the last surviving witness who appeared at the trail, and unless I reduce to writing what I happen to know, there will be no record of the true particulars left after my death.

In the town of Betminster, and round about it for many a good English mile, I am known as Dame Roundwood. I have never been married, and at my present age, I never shall be. My one living relative, at the past time of which I now write, was my sister—married to a man named Morcom. He was settled in France, as a breeder of horses. Now and then he crossed over to England on his business, and went back again.

I took such a dislike to Morcom that I refused to be present at the wedding. This led, of course, to a quarrel. Nephews and nieces, if there had been any, might perhaps have reconciled me with my sister. As it was, we never wrote to each other after she went to France with her husband. And I never saw her again until she lay on her deathbed. So much about myself, to begin with.

Circumstances, which it is neither needful nor pleasant to dwell on in this place, occasioned the loss of my income, while I was still in the prime of my life. I had no choice but to make the best of a bad bargain, and to earn my bread by going out to service.

Having provided myself with good recommendations, I applied for the vacant place of housekeeper to Farmer Fairweather. I had heard of him as a well-to-do old bachelor, cultivating his land nigh on five miles in a northerly direction beyond Betminster. But I positively declare that I had never been in his house, or exchanged a word with him, on the day when I set forth for the farm.

The door was opened to me by a nice little girl. I noticed that her manners were pretty, and her voice was a remarkably strong one for her age. She had, I may also mention, the finest blue eyes I ever saw in any young creature's face. When she looked at you, there was just a cast, as they call it, in her left eye, barely noticeable, and not a deformity in any sense of the word. The one drawback that I could find in this otherwise pleasing young person was that she had a rather sullen look, and that she seemed to be depressed in her spirits.

But, like most people the girl was ready enough to talk about herself. I found that her name was Dina Coomb, and that she had lost both her parents. Farmer Fairweather was her guardian, as well as her uncle, and held a fortune of ten thousand pounds ready and waiting for her when she came of age.

What would become of the money if she died in her youth was more than Dina could tell me. Her mother's timepiece had already been given to her, by directions in her mother's will. It looked of great value to my eyes, and it flattered her vanity to see how I admired her grand gold watch.

'I hope you are coming to stay here,' she said to me.

This seemed, as I thought, rather a sudden fancy to take to a stranger. 'Why do you want me to stay with you?' I asked.

And she hung her head, and had nothing to say. The farmer came in from his fields, and I entered on my business with him. At the same time I noticed, with some surprise, that Dina slipped out of the room by one door when her uncle came in by the other.

He was pleased with my recommendations, and he civilly offered me sufficient wages. Moreover, he was still fair to look upon, and not (as some farmers are) slovenly in his dress. So far from being an enemy to this miserable man, as has been falsely asserted, I gladly engaged to take my place at the farm on the next day at twelve o'clock, noon.

A friendly neighbour at Betminster, one Master Gouch, gave me a cast in his gig. We arrived true to the appointed time. While Master Gouch waited to bring my box after me, I opened the garden gate and rang the bell at the door. There was no answer. I had just rung once more, when I heard a scream in the house. There were words that followed the scream, in a voice which I recognized as the voice of Dina Coomb:

'Oh, uncle, don't kill me!'

I was too frightened to know what to do. Master Gouch, having heard that dreadful cry as I did, jumped out of the gig and tried the door. It was not fastened inside. Just as he was stepping over the threshold, the farmer bounced out of a room that opened into the passage, and asked what he did there.

My good neighbour answered, 'Here, sir, is Dame Roundwood, come to your house by your own appointment.'

Thereupon Farmer Fairweather said he had changed his mind, and meant to do without a housekeeper. He spoke in an angry manner, and he took the door in his hand, as if he meant to shut us out. But before he could do this, we heard a moaning in the room that he had just come out of. Says my neighbour,

'There's somebody hurt, I'm afraid.'

Says I, 'Is it your niece, sir?'

The farmer slammed the door in our faces, and then locked it against us. There was no help for it after this but to go back to Betminster.

Master Gouch, a cautious man in all things, recommended that we should wait awhile before we spoke of what had happened, on the chance of receiving an explanation and apology from the farmer when he recovered his temper. I agreed to this. But there! I am a woman, and I did take a lady (a particular friend of mine) into my confidence. The next day it was all over the town. Inquiries were made; some of the labourers on the farm said strange things; the mayor and aldermen heard of what was going on. When I next saw Farmer Fairweather he was charged with the murder of his niece, and I was called, along with Master Gouch and the labourers, as witnesses against him.

The ins and outs of the law are altogether beyond me. I can only report that Dina Coomb was certainly missing, and this, taken with what Master Gouch and I had heard and seen, was (as the lawyers said) the case against the farmer. His defence was that Dina was a bad girl. He found it necessary, standing towards her in the place of her father, to correct his niece with a leather strap from time to time; and we upset his temper by trying to get into his house when strangers were not welcome, and might misinterpret his actions. As for the disappearance of Dina, he could only conclude that she had run away, and where she had gone to was more than he had been able to discover.

To this the law answered, 'You have friends to help you, and you are rich enough to pay the expense of a strict search. Find Dina Coomb, and produce her here to prove what you have said. We will give you reasonable time. Make the best use of it.'

Ten days passed, and we, the witnesses, were summoned again. How it came out I don't know. Everybody in Betminster was talking of it; Farmer Fairweather's niece had been found.

The girl told her story, and the people who had discovered her told *their* story. It was all plain and straightforward, and I had just begun to wonder what I was wanted for, when up got the lawyer who had the farmer's interests in charge, and asked that the witnesses might be ordered to leave the court. We were turned out under the care of an usher; and we were sent for as the authorities wanted us, to speak to the identity of Dina, one at a time. The parson of Farmer Fairweather's parish church was the first witness called. Then came the turn of the labourers. I was sent for last.

When I had been sworn, and when the girl and I were, for the first time, set close together face to face, a most extraordinary interest seemed to be felt in my evidence. How I first came to be in Dina's company, and how long a time had passed while I was talking with her, were questions which I answered as I had answered them once already, ten days since.

When a voice warned me to be careful and to take my time, and another said. 'Is that Dina Coomb?' I was too much excited—I may even say, too much frightened—to turn my head and see who was speaking to me. The longer I looked at the girl, the more certain I felt that I was *not* looking at Dina.

What could I do? As an honest woman giving evidence on her oath I was bound, come what might of it, to tell the truth. To the voice which had asked me if that was Dina Coomb, I answered positively, 'No.'

My reasons when given, were two in number. First, both this girl's eyes were as straight as straight could be—not so much as the vestige of a cast could I see in her left eye. Secondly, she was fatter than Dina in the face, and fatter in the neck and arms, and rounder in the shoulders. I owned, when the lawyer put the question to me, that she was the same height as Dina, and had the same complexion and the same fine blue colour in her eyes. But I stuck fast to the differences I had noticed—and they said I turned the scale against the prisoner.

As I afterwards discovered, we witnesses had not been agreed. The labourers declared that the girl was Dina. The parson, who had seen Dina hundreds of times at his school, said exactly what I had said. Other competent witnesses were sought for and found the next day. Their testimony was our testimony repeated again and again. Later still, the abominable father and mother who had sold their child for purposes of deception were discovered, and were afterwards punished, along with the people who had paid the money.

Driven to the wall, the prisoner owned that he had failed to find his runaway niece; and that, in terror of being condemned to die on the scaffold for murder, he had made this desperate attempt to get himself acquitted by deceiving the law. His confession availed him nothing; his solemn assertion of innocence availed him nothing. Farmer Fairweather was hanged.

With the passing away of time the memory of things passes away too. I was beginning to be an old woman, and the trial was only remembered by elderly people like myself, when I got a letter relating to my sister. It was written for her by the English consul at the French town in which she lived. He informed me that she had been a widow for some years past; and he summoned me instantly to her bedside if I wished to see her again before she died.

I was just in time to find her living. She was past speaking to me but, thank God, she understood what I meant when I kissed her and asked her to forgive me. Towards evening the poor soul passed away quietly, with her head resting on my breast.

The consul had written down what she had wanted to say to me. I leave the persons who may read this to judge what my feelings were when I discovered that my sister's husband was the wretch who had assisted the escape of Dina Coomb, and who had thus been the means of condemning an innocent man to death on the scaffold.

On one of those visits on business to England of which I have already spoken, he had met a little girl sitting under a hedge at the side of the high road, lost, footsore, and frightened, and had spoken to her. She owned that she had run away from home after a most severe beating. She showed the marks. A worthy man would have put her under the protection of the nearest magistrate.

My rascally brother-in-law noticed her valuable watch, and, suspecting that she might be connected with wealthy people, he encouraged her to talk. When he was well assured of her expectations, and of the use to which he might put them in her friendless situation, he offered to adopt her, and he took her away with him to France.

My sister, having no child of her own took a liking to Dina, and readily believed what her husband chose to tell her. For three years the girl lived with them. She cared little for the good woman who was always kind to her, but she was most unreasonably fond of the villain who had kidnapped her.

After his death this runaway creature—then aged fifteen—was missing again. She left a farewell letter to my sister, saying that she had found another friend; and from that time forth nothing more had been heard of her, for years on years. This had weighed on my sister's mind, and this was what she had wanted to tell me on her deathbed. Knowing nothing of the trial, she was aware that Dina belonged to the neighbourhood of Betminster, and she thought in her ignorance that I might communicate with Dina's friends, if such persons existed.

On my return to England I thought it a duty to show to the Mayor of Betminster what the consul had written from my sister's dictation. He read it and heard what I had to tell him. Then he reckoned up the years that had passed. Says he, 'The girl must be of age by this time; I shall cause inquiries to be made in London.'

In a week more we did hear of Dina Coomb. She had returned to her own country, with a French husband at her heels, had proved her claim, and had got her money.

4

THE HIDDEN CASH

I

Parson Tibbald, a magistrate living within a day's ride of the ancient city of York, surprised the members of his family, one morning, by presenting himself at breakfast without an appetite. Upon his wife asking him if the dishes on the table were not to his taste, he answered, 'My day's work is not to my taste. For the first time since I have been one of his majesty's justices, a charge of murder is coming before me, and the man accused is one of our neighbours.'

The person in this miserable plight was Thomas Harris, an innkeeper, charged with murdering James Gray, a traveller sleeping in his house.

The witnesses against him were his own servants: Elias Morgan, variously employed as waiter, hostler and gardener; and Maria Mackling, chambermaid. In his evidence against his master, Morgan declared that he had seen Thomas Harris on the traveller's bed, killing the man by strangling. In fear of what might happen if he remained in the room, Morgan feigned to go downstairs. Returning secretly, he looked through the keyhole of a door in an adjoining bedchamber, and saw the landlord rifling James Gray's pockets.

Harris answered to this that all his neighbours knew him

to be an honest man. He had found Gray in a fit, and had endeavored to restore him to his senses without success. The doctor who had examined the body, supported this assertion by declaring that he had found no marks of violence on the dead traveller. In the opinion of the magistrate, the case against Harris had now broken down, and the prisoner would have been discharged, but for the appearance of the maidservant asking to be sworn.

Maria Mackling then made the statement that follows:

'On the morning when my fellow-servant found Mr Harris throttling James Gray, I was in the back wash-house, which looks out on the garden. I saw my master in the garden, and wondered what he wanted there at that early hour. I watched him. He was within a few yards of the window, when I saw him take a handful of gold pieces out of his pocket, and wrap them up in something that looked like a bit of canvas. After that, he went on to a tree in a corner of the garden, and dug a hole under the tree and hid the money in it. Send the constable with me to the garden, and let him see if I have not spoken the truth.'

But good Parson Tibbald waited awhile to give his neighbour an opportunity of answering the maidservant. Thomas Harris startled everybody present by turning pale, and failing to defend himself intelligently against the serious statement made by the girl. The constable was accordingly sent to the garden with Maria Mackling—and there, under the tree, the gold pieces were found. After this the magistrate had but one alternative left. He committed the prisoner for trial at the next assizes.

II

The witnesses having repeated their evidence before the judge and the jury, Thomas Harris was asked what he had to say in his own defence.

In those days the merciless law did not allow prisoners to have the assistance of counsel. Harris was left to do his best for himself. During his confinement in prison, he had found time to compose his mind, and to consider beforehand how he might most fitly plead his own cause. After a solemn assertion of his innocence, he proceeded in these words:

'At my examination before the magistrate, my maidservant's evidence took me by surprise. I was ashamed to acknowledge what I am now resolved to confess. My lord, I am by nature a covetous man, fond of money, afraid of thieves, and suspicious of people about me who know that I am well-to-do in the world. I admit that I did what other miserly men have done before me: I hid the gold as the girl has said. But I buried it in secret for my own better security. Every farthing of that money is my property, and has been honestly come by.'

Such was the defence in substance. Having heard it, the judge summed up the case.

His lordship dwelt particularly on the circumstance of the hiding of the money; pointing out the weakness of the reasons assigned by the prisoner for his conduct, and leaving it to the jury to decide which they believed—the statement given in evidence by the witnesses, or the statement made by Harris. The jury appeared to think consultation among themselves, in this case, a mere waste of time. In two minutes they found the prisoner guilty of the murder of James Gray.

In these days, if a man had been judicially condemned to death on doubtful evidence, after two minutes of consideration, our parliament and our press would have saved his life. In the bad old times Thomas Harris was hanged; meeting his fate with firmness, and declaring his innocence with his last breath.

III

Between five and six months after the date of the execution, an

Englishman who had been employed in foreign military service returned to his own country, after an absence of twelve years, and set himself to discover the members of his family who might yet be in the land of the living. This man was Antony Gray, a younger brother of the deceased James.

He succeeded in tracing his mother's sister and her husband, two childless old people in feeble health. From the husband, who had been present at the trial, but who had not been included among the witnesses, Antony heard the terrible story which has just been told. The evidence of the doctor and the defence of Thomas Harris produced a strong impression on him. He asked a question which ought to have been put at the trial:

'Was my brother James rich enough to have a handful of gold pieces about him, when he slept at the inn?'

The old man knew little or nothing of James and his affairs. The good wife, who was better informed, answered: 'He never, to my knowledge, had as much as a spare pound in his pocket at any time in his life.'

Antony, remembering the landlord's explanation of his brother's death, asked next if his aunt had ever heard that James was liable to fits. She confessed to a suspicion that James had suffered in that way. 'He and his mother,' she explained, 'kept this infirmity of my nephew's (if he had it) a secret. When they were both staying with us on a visit, he was found lying for dead in the road. His mother said, and he said, it was an accident caused by a fall. All I can tell you is that the doctor who brought him to his senses called it a fit.'

After considering a little with himself, Antony begged leave to put one question more. He asked for the name of the village in which the inn, once kept by Thomas Harris, was situated. Having received this information, he got up to say good-bye. His uncle and aunt wanted to know why he was leaving them in that sudden way.

To this he returned rather a strange answer: 'I have a fancy for making acquaintance with two of the witnesses at the trial, and I mean to try if I can hear of them in the village.'

IV

The manservant and the woman-servant who had been in the employment of Thomas Harris had good characters, and were allowed to keep their places by the person who succeeded to possession of the inn. Under the new proprietor the business had fallen off. The place was associated with a murder, and a prejudice against it existed in the minds of travellers. The bedrooms were all empty, one evening, when a stranger arrived, who described himself as an angler desirous of exercising his skill in the trout-stream which ran near the village.

He was a handsome man, still young, with pleasant manners, and with something in his fine upright figure which suggested to the new landlord that he might have been at one time in the army. Everybody in the village liked him; he spent his money freely, and he was especially kind and considerate towards the servants.

Elias Morgan frequently accompanied him on his fishing excursions. Maria Mackling looked after his linen with extraordinary care, contrived to meet him constantly on the stairs, and greatly enjoyed the compliments which the handsome gentleman paid to her on those occasions.

In the exchange of confidences that followed, he told Maria that he was a single man, and he was thereupon informed that the chambermaid and the waiter were engaged to be married. They were only waiting to find better situations, and to earn money enough to start in business for themselves.

In the third week of the stranger's residence at the inn, there occurred a change for the worse in his relations with one of the two servants. He excited the jealousy of Elias Morgan.

This man set himself to watch Maria, and made discoveries which so enraged him that he not only behaved with brutality to his affianced wife, but forgot the respect due to his master's guest. The amiable gentleman, who had shown such condescending kindness towards his inferiors, suddenly exhibited a truculent temper. He knocked the waiter down. Elias got up again with an evil light in his eyes. He said, 'The man who once kept this house knocked me down, and he lived, sir, to be sorry for it.'

Self-betrayed by those threatening words, Elias went out of the room.

Having discovered in this way that his suspicions of one of the witnesses against the unfortunate Harris had been well founded, Antony Gray set his trap next to catch the woman, and achieved a result which he had not ventured to contemplate.

Having obtained a private interview with Maria Mackling, he presented himself in the character of a penitent man. 'I am afraid,' he said, 'that I have innocently lowered you in the estimation of your jealous sweetheart. I shall never forgive myself, if I have been so unfortunate as to raise an obstacle to your marriage.'

Maria rewarded the handsome, single gentleman with a look which expressed modest anxiety to obtain a position in *his* estimation.

'I must forgive you, if you can't forgive yourself,' she answered, softly. 'Indeed, I owe you a debt of gratitude. You have released me from an engagement to a brute. And, what is more,' she added, beginning to lose her temper, 'an ungrateful brute. But for me, Elias Morgan might have been put in prison, and have richly deserved it!'

Antony did his best to persuade her to speak more plainly. But Maria was on her guard and plausibly deferred explanation to a future opportunity. She had, nevertheless, said enough already to lead to serious consequences.

The jealous waiter, still a self-appointed spy on Maria's movements, had heard in hiding all that passed at the interview. Partly in revenge, partly in his own interests, he decided on anticipating any confession on the chambermaid's part. The same day he presented himself before Parson Tibbald as a repentant criminal, resigned to enlighten justice in the character of King's Evidence.

V

The infamous conspiracy to which Thomas Harris had fallen a victim had been first suggested by his own miserly habits.

Purely by accident, in the first instance, the woman-servant had seen him secretly burying money under the tree, and had informed the manservant of her discovery.

He had examined the hiding-place, with a view to robbery which might benefit his sweetheart and himself, and had found the sum secreted too small to be worth the risk of committing theft. Biding their time, he and his accomplice privately watched the additions made to their master's store. On the day when James Gray slept at the inn, they found gold enough to tempt them at last.

How to try the experiment of theft without risk of discovery was the one difficulty that presented itself. In this emergency, Elias Morgan conceived the diabolical scheme of charging Harris with the murder of the traveller who had died in a fit. The failure of the false evidence, and the prospect of the prisoner's discharge, terrified Maria Mackling.

Elias had placed himself in a position which threatened him with indictment for perjury. The woman claimed to be heard as a witness, and deliberately sacrificed her master on the scaffold to secure the safety of her accomplice.

The two wretches were committed to prison. It is not often

that poetical justice punishes crime, out of the imaginary court of appeal which claims our sympathies on the stage. But, in this case, retribution did really overtake atrocious guilt. Elias Morgan and Maria Mackling both died in prison of the disease then known as gaol fever.

5

NINE O'CLOCK

The night of the 30th of June, 1793, is memorable in the prison annals of Paris as the last night in confinement of the leaders of the famous Girondin party in the first French revolution. On the morning of the 31st, the twenty-one deputies, who represented the department of the Gironde, were guillotined to make way for Robespierre and the Reign of Terror.

With these men fell the last revolutionists of that period who shrank from founding a republic on massacre; who recoiled from substituting for a monarchy of corruption, a monarchy of bloodshed. The elements of their defeat lay as much in themselves, as in the events of their time. They were not, as a party, true to their own convictions; they temporized; they fatally attempted to take a middle course amid the terrible emergencies of a terrible epoch, and they fell—fell before worse men, because those men were in earnest.

Condemned to die, the Girondins submitted nobly to their fate; their great glory was the glory of their deaths. The speech of one of them, on hearing his sentence pronounced, was a prophecy of the future, fulfilled to the letter.

'*I die*,' he said to the Jacobin judges, the creatures of Robespierre, who tried him. '*I die at a time when the people have lost their reason; *you* will die on the day when they recover it.' Valazé was the only member of the condemned party who displayed a momentary weakness; he stabbed himself on hearing his sentence pronounced. But the blow was not mortal—he died on the scaffold, and died bravely with the rest.

On the night of the 30th the Girondins held their famous banquet in the prison; celebrated, with the ferocious stoicism of the time, their last social meeting before the morning on which they were to die. Other men, besides the twenty-one, were present at this supper of the condemned. They were prisoners who held Girondin opinions, but whose names were not illustrious enough for history to preserve. Though sentenced to confinement they were not sentenced to death. Some of their number, who had protested most boldly against the condemnation of the deputies, were ordered to witness the execution on the morrow, as a timely example to terrify them into submission. More than this, Robespierre and his colleagues did not, as yet, venture to attempt: the Reign of Terror was a cautious reign at starting.

The supper table of the prison was spread; the guests, twenty-one of their number stamped already with the seal of death, were congregated at the last Girondin banquet; toast followed toast; the *Marseillaise* was sung; the desperate triumph of the feast was rising fast to its climax, when a new and ominous subject of conversation was started at the lower end of the table, and spread electrically, almost in a moment, to the top.

This subject (by whom originated no one knew) was simply a question as to the hour in the morning at which the execution was to take place. Every one of the prisoners appeared to be in ignorance on this point; and the gaolers either could not, or would not, enlighten them. Until the cart for the condemned rolled into the prison yard, not one of the Girondins could tell whether he was to be called out to the guillotine soon after sunrise, or not till near noon.

This uncertainty was made a topic for discussion, or for jesting, on all sides. It was eagerly seized on as a pretext for raising to the highest pitch the ghastly animation and hilarity of the evening. In some quarters, the recognized hour of former executions was quoted as precedent sure to be followed by the executioners of the morrow; in others, it was asserted that Robespierre and his party would purposely depart from established customs in this, as in previous instances. Dozens of wild schemes were suggested for guessing the hour by fortune-telling rules on the cards; bets were offered and accepted among the prisoners who were not condemned to death, and witnessed in stoical mockery by the prisoners who were. Jests were exchanged about early rising and hurried toilets; in short, every man contributed an assertion, with one solitary exception. That exception was the Girondin, Duprat, one of the deputies who was sentenced to die by the guillotine.

He was a younger man than the majority of his brethren, and was personally remarkable by his pale, handsome, melancholy face, and his reserved yet gentle manners. Throughout the evening, he had spoken but rarely; there was something of the silence and serenity of a martyr in his demeanour. That he feared death as little as any of his companions was plainly visible in his bright, steady eye; in his unchanging complexion; in his firm, calm voice, when he occasionally addressed those who happened to be near him. But he was evidently out of place at the banquet; his temperament was reflective, his disposition serious; feasts were at no time a sphere in which he was calculated to shine.

His taciturnity, while the hour of the execution was under discussion, had separated him from most of those with whom he sat, at the lower end of the table. They edged up towards the top, where the conversation was most general and most animated. One of his friends, however, still kept his place by Duprat's side, and thus questioned him anxiously, but in low tones, on the cause of his immovable silence:

'Are you the only man of the company, Duprat, who has neither a guess nor a joke to make about the time of the execution?'

'I never joke, Marginy,' was the answer, given with a slight smile which had something of the sarcastic in it; 'and as for guessing at the time of the execution, I never guess at things which I *know*.'

'Know! You know the hour of the execution! Then why not communicate your knowledge to your friends around you?'

'Because not one of them would believe what I said.'

'But, surely, you could prove it. Somebody must have told you.'

'Nobody has told me.'

'You have seen some private letter, then; or you have managed to get sight of the execution order; or—'

'Spare your conjectures, Marginy. I have not read, as I have not been told, what is the hour at which we are to die tomorrow.'

'Then how on earth can you possibly know it?'

'I do *not* know when the execution will begin, or when it will end. I only know that it will be *going on* at nine o'clock tomorrow morning. Out of the twenty-one who are to suffer death, one will be guillotined exactly at that hour. Whether he will be the first whose head falls, or the last, I cannot tell.'

'And pray who may this man be, who is going to die exactly at nine o'clock? Of course, prophetically knowing so much, you know that!'

'I *do* know it. I am the man whose death by the guillotine will take place exactly at the hour I have mentioned.'

'You said just now, Duprat, that you never joked. Do you expect me to believe that what you have just spoken is spoken in earnest?'

'I repeat that I never joke; and I answer that I expect you to believe me. I know the hour at which my death will take place tomorrow, just as certainly as I know the fact of my own existence tonight.'

'But how? My dear friend, can you really lay claim to supernatural intuition, in this eighteenth century of the world, in this renowned Age of Reason?'

'No two men, Marginy, understand that word, supernatural, exactly in the same sense; you and I differ about its meaning, or, in other words, differ about the real distinction between the doubtful and the true. We will not discuss the subject: I wish to be understood, at the outset, as laying claim to no superior intuitions whatever; but I tell you, at the same time, that even in this Age of Reason, I have reason for what I have said. My father and my brother both died at nine o'clock in the morning, and were both warned very strangely of their deaths. I am the last of my family; I was warned last night, as they were warned; and I shall die by the guillotine, as they died in their beds, at the fatal hour of nine.'

'But, Duprat, why have I never heard of this before? As your oldest and, I am sure, your dearest friend, I thought you had long since trusted me with all your secrets.'

'And you shall know this secret; I only kept it from you till the time when I would be certain that my death would substantiate my words, to the very letter. Come! you are as bad supper company as I am; let us slip away from the table unperceived, while our friends are all engaged in conversation. Yonder end of the hall is dark and quiet—we can speak there uninterruptedly, for some hours to come,'

He led the way from the supper table, followed by Marginy.

Arrived at one of the darkest and most retired corners of the great hall of the prison, Duprat spoke again:

'I believe, Marginy,' he said, 'that you are one of those who have been ordered by our tyrants to witness my execution, and the execution of my brethren, as a warning spectacle for an enemy to the Jacobin cause?'

'My dear, dear friend! it is too true; I am ordered to witness the butchery which I cannot prevent—our last awful parting will be at the foot of the scaffold. I am among the victims who are spared—mercilessly spared—for a little while yet.'

'Say the martyrs! We die as martyrs, calmly, hopefully, innocently. When I am placed under the guillotine tomorrow morning, listen, my friend, for the striking of the church clocks; listen for the hour while you look your last on me. Until that time, suspend your judgment on the strange chapter of family history which I am now about to relate.'

Marginy took his friend's hand, and promised compliance with the request. Duprat then began as follows:

'You knew my brother Alfred, when he was quite a youth, and you knew something of what people flippantly termed the eccentricities of his character. He was three years my junior; but from childhood, he showed far less of a child's innate levity and happiness than his elder brother. He was noted for his seriousness and thoughtfulness as a boy; showed little inclination for a boy's usual lessons, and less still for a boy's usual recreations—in short, he was considered by everybody (my father included) as deficient in intellect; as a vacant dreamer, and an inveterate idler, whom it was hopeless to improve. Our tutor tried to lead him to various studies, and tried in vain. It was the same when the cultivation of his mind was given up, and the cultivation of his body was next attempted. The fencing master could make nothing of him; and the dancing master, after the first three lessons, resigned in despair. Seeing that it was useless to set others to teach him, my father made a virtue of necessity, and left him, if he chose, to teach himself.

'To the astonishment of every one, he had not been long consigned to his own guidance when he was discovered in the library, reading every old treatise on astrology which he could lay his hands on. He had rejected all useful knowledge for the most obsolete of obsolete sciences—the old, abandoned delusion of divination by stars! My father laughed heartily over the strange study to which his idle son had at last applied himself, but made no attempt to oppose his new caprice, and sarcastically presented him with a telescope on his next birthday. I should remind you here, of what you may perhaps have forgotten, that my father was a philosopher of the Voltaire school, who believed that the summit of human wisdom was to arrive at the power of sneering at all enthusiasms, and doubting of all truths. Apart from his philosophy, he was a kind-hearted, easy man, of quick, rather than profound intelligence. He could see nothing in my brother's new occupation, but the evidence of a new idleness, a fresh caprice which would be abandoned in a few months. My father was not the man to appreciate those yearnings towards the poetical and the spiritual, which were part of Alfred's temperament, and which gave to his peculiar studies of the stars and their influences a certain charm altogether unconnected with the more practical attractions of scientific investigation.

'This idle caprice of my brother's, as my father insisted on terming it, had lasted more than a twelvemonth, when there occurred the first of a series of mysterious and—as I consider them—supernatural events, with all of which Alfred was very remarkably connected. I was myself a witness of the strange circumstance, which I am now about to relate to you.

'One day—my brother being then sixteen years of age—I happened to go into my father's study, during his absence, and found Alfred there, standing close to a window, which looked into the garden. I walked up to him, and observed a curious expression of vacancy and rigidity in his face, especially in his eyes. Although I knew him to be subject to what are called fits of absence, I still thought it rather extraordinary that he never moved, and never noticed me when I was close to him. I took his hand, and asked if he was unwell. His flesh felt quite cold; neither my touch nor my voice produced the smallest sensation in him. Almost at the same moment when I noticed this, I happened to be looking accidentally towards the garden. There was my father walking along one of the paths, and there, by his side, walking with him, was *another Alfred!*—Another, yet exactly the same as the Alfred by whose side I was standing, whose hand I still held in mine!

'Thoroughly panic-stricken, I dropped his hand, and uttered a cry of terror. At the loud sound of my voice, the statue-like presence before me immediately began to show signs of animation. I looked round again at the garden. The figure of my brother, which I had beheld there, was gone, and I saw, to my horror, that my father was looking for it—looking in all directions for the companion (spectre, or human being?) of his walk!

'When I turned towards Alfred once more, he had (if I may so express it) come to life again, and was asking, with his usual gentleness of manner and kindness of voice, why I was looking so pale? I evaded the question by making some excuse, and in my turn inquired of him how long he had been in my father's study.

'"Surely you ought to know best," he answered with a laugh, "for you must have been here before me. It is not many minutes ago since I was walking in the garden with—"

'Before he could complete the sentence my father entered the room.

'"Oh! here you are, Master Alfred," said he. "May I ask for what purpose you took it into your wise head to vanish in that extraordinary manner? Why you slipped away from me in an instant, while I was picking a flower! On my word, sir, you're a better player at hide-and-seek than your brother—*he* would only have run into the shrubbery, *you* have managed to run in here, though how you did it in the time passes my poor comprehension. I was not a moment picking the flower, yet in that moment you were gone!"

'Alfred glanced suddenly and searchingly at me; his face became deadly pale, and, without speaking a word, he hurried from the room.

'"Can *you* explain this?" said my father, looking very much astonished.

'I hesitated a moment, and then told him what I had seen. He took a pinch of snuff—a favourite habit with him when he was going to be sarcastic, in imitation of Voltaire.

'"One visionary in a family is enough," said he; "I recommend you not to turn yourself into a bad imitation of your brother Alfred! Send your ghost after me, my good boy! I am going back into the garden, and should like to see him again!"

'Ridicule, even much sharper than this, would have had little effect on me. If I was certain of anything in the world, I was certain that I had seen my brother in the study—nay, more, had touched him—and equally certain that I had seen his double—his exact similitude, in the garden. As far as any man could know that he was in possession of his own senses, I knew myself to be in possession of mine. Left alone to think over what I had beheld, I felt a supernatural terror creeping through me—a terror which increased, when I recollected that, on one or two occasions, friends had said they had seen Alfred out of doors, when we all knew him to be at home. These statements, which my father had laughed at, and had taught me to laugh at, either as a trick, or a delusion on the part of others, now recurred to my memory as startling corroborations of what I had just seen myself. The solitude of the study oppressed me in a manner which I cannot describe. I left the apartment to seek Alfred, determined to question him, with all possible caution, on the subject of his strange trance, and his sensations at the moment when I had awakened him from it.

'I found him in his bedroom, still pale, and now very thoughtful. As the first words in reference to the scene in the study passed my lips, he started violently, and entreated me, with very unusual warmth of speech and manner, never to speak to him on that subject again—never, if I had any love or regard for him! Of course, I complied with his request. The mystery, however, was not destined to end here.

'About two months after the event which I have just related, we had arranged, one evening, to go to the theatre. My father had insisted that Alfred should be of the party, otherwise he would certainly have declined accompanying us; for he had no inclination whatever for public amusements of any kind. However, with his usual docility, he prepared to obey my father's desire, by going upstairs to put on his evening dress. It was wintertime, so he was obliged to take a candle with him.

'We waited in the drawing room for his return a very long time, so long that my father was on the point of sending upstairs to remind him of the lateness of the hour, when Alfred reappeared without the candle which he had taken with him from the room. The ghostly alteration over his face—the hideous, death-look that distorted his features I shall never forget—I shall see it tomorrow on the scaffold!

'Before either my father or I could utter a word, my brother said, "I have been taken suddenly ill; but I am better now. Do you still wish me to go to the theatre?"

"Certainly not, my dear Alfred," answered my father; "we must send for the doctor immediately."

"'Pray do not call in the doctor, sir; he would be of no use. I will tell you why, if you will let me speak to you alone."

'My father, looking seriously alarmed, signed to me to leave the room. For more than half an hour I remained absent, suffering almost unendurable suspense and anxiety on my brother's account. When I was recalled, I observed that Alfred was quite calm, though still deadly pale. My father's manner displayed an agitation which I had never observed in it before. He rose from his chair when I re-entered the room, and left me alone with my brother.

"'Promise me," said Alfred, in answer to my entreaties to know what had happened, "promise that you will not ask me to tell you more than my father has permitted me to tell. It is his desire that I should keep certain things a secret from you."

'I gave the required promise, but gave it most unwillingly. Alfred then proceeded:

"'When I left you to go and dress for the theatre, I felt a sense of oppression all over me, which I cannot describe. As soon as I was alone, it seemed as if some part of the life within me was slowly wasting away. I could hardly breathe the air around me, big drops of perspiration burst out on my forehead, and then a feeling of terror seized me which I was utterly unable to control. Some of those strange fancies of seeing my mother's spirit, which used to influence me at the time of her death, came back again to my mind. I ascended the stairs slowly and painfully, not daring to look behind me, for I heard—yes, heard!—something following me. When I got into my room and had shut the door, I began to recover my self-possession a little. But the sense of oppression was still as heavy on me as ever, when I approached the wardrobe to get out my clothes. Just as I stretched forth my hand to turn the key, I saw, to my horror, the two doors of the wardrobe opening of themselves, opening slowly and silently. The candle went out at the same moment, and the whole inside of the wardrobe became to me like a great mirror, with a bright light shining in the middle of it. Out of that light there came a figure, the exact counterpart of myself. Over its breast hung an open scroll, and on that I read the warning of my own death, and a revelation of the destinies of my father and his race. Do not ask me what were the words on the scroll, I have given my promise not to tell you. I may only say that, as soon as I had read all, the room grew dark, and the vision disappeared."

'Forgetful of my promise, I entreated Alfred to repeat to me the words on the scroll. He smiled sadly, and refused to speak on the subject any more. I next sought out my father, and begged him to divulge the secret. Still sceptical to the last, he answered that one diseased imagination in the family was enough, and that he would not permit me to run the risk of being infected by Alfred's mental malady. I passed the whole of that day and the next in a state of agitation and alarm which nothing could tranquillize. The sight I had seen in the study gave a terrible significance to the little that my brother had told me. I was uneasy if he was a moment out of my sight. There was something in his expression—calm and even cheerful as it was—which made me dread the worst.

'On the morning of the third day after the occurrence I have just related, I rose very early, after a sleepless night, and went into Alfred's bedroom. He was awake, and welcomed me with more than usual affection and kindness. As I drew a chair to his bedside, he asked me to get pen, ink, and paper, and write down something from his dictation. I obeyed, and found, to my terror and distress, that the idea of death was more present to his imagination than ever. He employed me in writing a statement of his wishes in regard to the disposal of all his own little possessions, as keepsakes to be given, after he was no more, to my father, myself, the house servants, and one or two of his own most intimate friends. Over and over again, I entreated him to tell me whether he really believed that his death was near. He invariably replied that I should soon know, and then led the conversation to indifferent topics. As the morning advanced, he asked to see my father, who came, accompanied by the doctor, the latter having been in attendance for the last two days.

'Alfred took my father's hand, and begged his forgiveness of any offence, any disobedience of which he had ever been guilty. Then, reaching out his other hand, and taking mine, as I stood on the opposite side of the bed, he asked what the time was. A clock was placed on the mantelpiece of the room, but not in a position in which he could see it, as he now lay. I turned round to look at the dial, and answered that it was just on the stroke of nine.

"'Farewell!" said Alfred, calmly; "in this world, farewell for ever!"

'The next instant the clock struck. I felt his fingers tremble in mine, then grow quite still. The doctor seized a hand-mirror that lay on the table, and held it over his lips. He was dead—dead, as the last chime of the hour echoed through the awful silence of the room!

'I pass over the first days of our affliction. You, who have suffered the loss of a beloved sister, can well imagine their misery. I pass over these days, and pause for a moment at the time when we could speak with some calmness and resignation on the subject of our bereavement. On the arrival of that period, I ventured, in conversation with my father, to refer to the vision which had been seen by our dear Alfred in his bedroom, and to the prophecy which he described himself as having read upon the supernatural scroll.

'Even yet my father persisted in his scepticism; but now, as it seemed to me, more because he was afraid, than because he was unwilling, to believe. I again recalled to his memory what I myself had seen in the study. I asked him to recollect how certain Alfred had been beforehand, and how fatally right, about the day and hour of his death. Still I could get but one answer; my brother had died of a nervous disorder (the doctor said so); his imagination had been diseased from his childhood; there was only one way of treating the vision which he described himself as having seen, and that was not to speak of it again between ourselves; never to speak of it at all to our friends.

'We were sitting in the study during this conversation. It was evening. As my father uttered the last words of his reply to me, I saw his eye turn suddenly and uneasily towards the further end of the room. In dead silence, I looked in the same direction, and saw the door opening of itself. The vacant space beyond was filled with a bright, steady glow, which hid all outer objects in the hall, and which I cannot describe to you by likening it to any light that we are accustomed to behold either by day or night. In my terror, I caught my father by the arm, and asked him, in a whisper, whether he did not see something extraordinary in the direction of the doorway?

'"Yes," he answered, in tones as low as mine, "I see, or fancy I see, a strange light. The subject on which we have been speaking has impressed our feelings as it should not. Our nerves are still unstrung by the shock of the bereavement we have suffered: our senses are deluding us. Let us look away towards the garden."

'"But the opening of the door, father; remember the opening of the door!"

'"Ours is not the first door which has accidentally flown open of itself."

'"Then why not shut it again?"

'"Why not, indeed. I will close it at once." He rose, advanced a few paces, then stopped, and came back to his place. "It is a warm evening," he said, avoiding my eyes, which were eagerly fixed on him, "the room will be all the cooler, if the door is suffered to remain open."

'His face grew quite pale as he spoke. The light lasted for a few minutes longer, then suddenly disappeared. For the rest of the evening my father's manner was very much altered. He was silent and thoughtful, and complained of a feeling of oppression and languor, which he tried to persuade himself was produced by the heat of the weather. At an unusually early hour he retired to his room.

'The next morning, when I got downstairs, I found, to my astonishment, that the servants were engaged in preparations for the departure of somebody from the house. I made inquiries of one of them who was hurriedly packing a trunk. "My master, sir, starts for Lyons the first thing this morning," was the reply. I immediately repaired to my father's room, and found him there with an open letter in his hand, which he was reading. His face, as he looked up at me on my entrance, expressed the most violent emotions of apprehension and despair.

'"I hardly know whether I am awake or dreaming; whether I am the dupe of a terrible delusion, or the victim of a supernatural reality more terrible still," he said in low awestruck tones as I approached him. "One of the prophecies, which Alfred told me in private that he had read upon the scroll, has come true! He predicted the loss of the bulk of my fortune—here is the letter, which informs me that the merchant at Lyons, in whose hands my money was placed, has become bankrupt. Can the occurrence of this ruinous calamity be the chance fulfilment of a mere guess? Or was the doom of my family really revealed to my dead son? I go to Lyons immediately to know the truth: this letter may have been written under false information; it may be the work of an impostor. And yet, Alfred's prediction—I shudder to think of it!"

'"The light, father!" I exclaimed, "the light we saw last night in the study!"

'"Hush! don't speak of it! Alfred said that I should be warned of the truth of the prophecy, and of its immediate fulfilment, by the shining of the same supernatural light that he had seen—I tried to disbelieve what I beheld last night—I hardly know whether I dare believe it even now! This prophecy is not the last: there are others yet to be fulfilled—but let us not speak, let us not think of them! I must start at once for Lyons; I must be on the spot, if this horrible news is true, to save what I can from the wreck. The letter—give me back the letter!—I must go directly!"

'He hurried back from the room. I followed him; and, with some difficulty, obtained permission to be the companion of his momentous journey. When we arrived at Lyons, we found that the statement in the letter was true. My father's fortune was gone: a mere pittance, derived from a small estate that had belonged to my mother, was all that was left to us.

'My father's health gave way under this misfortune. He never referred again to Alfred's prediction, and I was afraid to mention the subject; but I saw that it was affecting his mind quite as painfully as the loss of his property. Over and over again, he checked himself very strangely when he was on the point of speaking to me about my brother. I saw that there was some secret pressing heavily on his mind, which he was afraid to disclose to me. It was useless to ask for his confidence. His temper had become irritable under disaster; perhaps, also, under the dread uncertainties which were now evidently tormenting him in secret. My situation was a very sad, and a very dreary one, at that time: I had no remembrances of the past that were not mournful and affrighting remembrances; I had no hopes for the future that were not darkened by a vague presentiment of troubles and perils to come; and I was expressly forbidden by my father to say a word about the terrible events, which had cast an unnatural gloom over my youthful career, to any of the friends (yourself included) whose counsel and whose sympathy might have guided and sustained me in the day of trial.

'We returned to Paris; sold our house there; and retired to live on the small estate, to which I have referred, as the last possession left us. We had not been many days in our new abode, when my father imprudently exposed himself to a heavy shower of rain, and suffered in consequence from a violent attack of cold. This temporary malady was not dreaded by the medical attendant; but it was soon aggravated by a fever, produced as much by the anxiety and distress of mind from which he continued to suffer, as by any other cause. Still the doctor gave hope; but still he grew daily worse—so much worse that I removed my bed into his room, and never quitted him night or day.

'One night I had fallen asleep, overpowered by fatigue and anxiety, when I was awakened by a cry from my father. I instantly trimmed the light, and ran to his side. He was sitting up in bed, with his eyes fixed on the door, which had been left ajar to ventilate the room. I saw nothing in that direction, and asked what was the matter. He murmured some expressions of affection towards me, and begged me to sit by his bedside till the morning; but gave no definite answer to my question. Once or twice, I thought he wandered a little; and I observed that he occasionally moved his hand under the pillow, as if searching for something there. However, when the morning came, he appeared to be calm and self-possessed. The doctor arrived; and pronouncing him to be better, retired to the dressing-room to write a prescription. The moment his back was turned, my father laid his weak hand on my arm, and whispered faintly:

"Last night I saw the supernatural light again—the second prediction—true, true—my death this time—the same hour as Alfred's—nine—nine o'clock, this morning." He paused a moment through weakness; then added: "Take that sealed paper—under the pillow—when I am dead, read it—now go into the dressing-room—my watch is there—I have heard the church clock strike eight; let me see how long it is now till nine—go—go quickly!"

'Horror-stricken, moving and acting like a man in a trance, I silently obeyed him. The doctor was still in the dressing-room: despair made me catch eagerly at any chance of saving my father; I told his medical attendant what I had just heard, and entreated advice and assistance without delay.

'"He is a little delirious," said the doctor—"don't be alarmed: we can cheat him out of his dangerous idea, and so perhaps save his life. Where is the watch?" (I produced it)—"See: it is ten minutes to nine. I will put back the hands one hour; that will give good time for a composing draught to operate. There! take him the watch, and let him see the false time with his own eyes. He will be comfortably asleep before the hour hand gets round again to nine."

'I went back with the watch to my father's bedside. "Too slow," he murmured, as he looked at the dial—"too slow by an hour—the church clock—I counted eight."

'"Father! dear father! you are mistaken," I cried, "*I* counted also: it was only seven."

'"Only seven!" he echoed faintly, "another hour then—another hour to live!" He evidently believed what I had said to him. In spite of the fatal experiences of the past, I now ventured to hope the best for our stratagem, as I resumed my place by his side.

'The doctor came in; but my father never noticed him. He kept his eyes fixed on the watch, which lay between us, on the coverlid. When the minute hand was within a few seconds of indicating the false hour of eight, he looked round at me, murmured very feebly and doubtingly, "Another hour to live!" and then gently closed his eyes. I looked at the watch, and saw that it was just eight o'clock, according to our alteration of the right time. At the same moment, I heard the doctor, whose hand had been on my father's pulse, exclaim, "My God! it's stopped! He *has* died at nine o'clock!"

'The fatality, which no human stratagem or human science could turn aside, was accomplished! I was alone in the world!

'In the solitude of our little cottage, on the day of my father's burial, I opened the sealed letter, which he had told me to take from the pillow of his deathbed. In preparing to read it, I knew that I was preparing for the knowledge of my own doom; but I neither trembled nor wept. I was beyond grief: despair, such as mine was then, is calm and self-possessed to the last.

'The letter ran thus: "After your father and brother have fallen under the fatality that pursues our house, it is right, my dear son, that you should be warned how *you* are included in the last of the predictions which still remains unaccomplished. Know then, that the final lines read by our dear Alfred on the scroll prophesied that *you* should die, as *we* have died, at the fatal hour of nine; but by a bloody and violent death, the day of which was not foretold. My beloved boy! you know not, you never will know, what I suffered in the possession of this terrible secret, as the truth of the former prophecies forced itself more and more plainly on my mind! Even now, as I write, I hope against all hope; believe vainly and desperately against all experience, that this last, worst doom may be avoided. Be cautious; be patient; look well before you at each step of your career. The fatality by which you are threatened is terrible; but there is a Power above fatality; and before that Power my spirit and my child's spirit now pray for you. Remember this when your heart is heavy, your path through life grows dark. Remember that the better world is still before you, the world where we shall all meet! Farewell!"

'When I first read those lines, I read them with the gloomy, immovable resignation of the Eastern fatalists; and that resignation never left me afterwards. Here, in this prison, I feel it, calm as ever. I bowed patiently to my doom, when it was only predicted; I bow to it as patiently now, when it is on the eve of accomplishment. You have often wondered, my friend, at the tranquil, equable sadness of my manner: after what I have just told you, can you wonder any longer?

'But let me return for a moment to the past. Though I had no hope of escaping the fatality which had overtaken my father and my brother, my life, after my double bereavement, was the existence of all others which might seem most likely to evade the accomplishment of my predicted doom. Yourself and one other friend excepted, I saw no society; my walks were limited to the cottage garden and the neighbouring fields, and my everyday, unvarying occupation was confined to that hard and resolute course of study, by which alone I could hope to prevent my mind from dwelling on what I had suffered in the past, or on what I might still be condemned to suffer in the future. Never was there a life more quiet and more uneventful than mine!

'You know how I awoke to an ambition, which irresistibly impelled me to change this mode of existence. News from Paris penetrated even to my obscure retreat, and disturbed my self-imposed tranquillity. I heard of the last errors and weaknesses of Louis the Sixteenth; I heard of the assembling of the States-General; and I knew that the French Revolution had begun. The tremendous emergencies of that epoch drew men of all characters from private to public pursuits, and made politics the necessity rather than the choice of every Frenchman's life. The great change preparing for the country acted universally on individuals, even to the humblest, and it acted on *me*.

'I was elected a deputy, more for the sake of the name I bore than on account of any little influence which my acquirements and my character might have exercised in the neighbourhood of my country abode. I removed to Paris, and took my seat in the Chamber, little thinking, at that time, of the crime and the bloodshed to which our revolution, so moderate in its beginning, would lead; little thinking that I had taken the first, irretrievable steps towards the bloody and violent death which was lying in store for me.

'Need I go on? You know how warmly I joined the Girondin party; you know how we have been sacrificed; you know what the death is which I and my brethren are to suffer tomorrow. On now ending, I repeat what I said at beginning: Judge not of my narrative till you have seen with your own eyes what really takes place in the morning. I have carefully abstained from all comment; I have simply related events as they happened, forbearing to add my own views of their significance, my own ideas on the explanation of which they admit. You may believe us to have been a family of nervous visionaries, witnesses of certain remarkable contingencies; victims of curious, but not impossible chances, which we have fancifully and falsely interpreted into supernatural events. I leave you undisturbed in this conviction (if you really feel it); tomorrow you will think differently; tomorrow you will be an altered man. In the meantime, remember what I now say, as you would remember my dying words: Last night I saw the supernatural radiance which warned my father and my brother; and which warns *me* that, whatever the time when the execution begins, whatever the order in which the twenty-one Girondins are chosen for death, I shall be the man who kneels under the guillotine, as the clock strikes nine!'

It was morning. Of the ghastly festivities of the night no sign remained. The prison hall wore an altered look, as the twenty-one condemned men (followed by those who were ordered to witness their execution) were marched out to the carts appointed to take them from the dungeon to the scaffold.

The sky was cloudless, the sun warm and brilliant, as the Girondin leaders and their companions were drawn slowly through the streets to the place of execution. Duprat and Marginy were placed in separate vehicles: the contrast in their demeanour at that awful moment was strongly marked. The features of the doomed man still preserved their noble and melancholy repose; his glance was steady; his colour never changed. The face of Marginy, on the contrary, displayed the strongest agitation; he was pale even to his lips. The terrible narrative he had heard, the anticipation of the final and appalling proof by which its truth was now to be tested, had robbed him, for the first time in his life, of all his self-possession. Duprat had predicted truly; the morrow had come, and he was an altered man already.

The carts drew up at the foot of the scaffold which was soon to be stained with the blood of twenty-one human beings. The condemned deputies mounted it; and ranged themselves at the end opposite the guillotine. The prisoners who were to behold the execution remained in their cart. Before Duprat ascended the steps, he took his friend's hand for the last time: 'Farewell!' he said, calmly. 'Farewell! I go to my father, and my brother! Remember my words of last night.'

With straining eyes, and bloodless cheeks, Marginy saw Duprat take his position in the middle row of his companions, who stood in three ranks of seven each. Then the awful spectacle of the execution began. After the first seven deputies had suffered there was a pause; the horrible traces of the judicial massacre were being removed. When the execution proceeded, Duprat was the third taken from the middle rank of the condemned. As he came forward, he stood for an instant erect under the guillotine. He looked with a smile on his friend, and repeated in a clear voice the word, *'Remember!'*—then bowed himself on the block. The blood stood still at Marginy's heart, as he looked and listened, during the moment of silence that followed. That moment past, the church clocks of Paris struck. He dropped down in the cart, and covered his face with his hands; for through the heavy beat of the hour he heard the fall of the fatal steel.

'Pray, sir, was it nine or ten that struck just now?' said one of Marginy's fellow prisoners to an officer of the guard who stood near the cart.

The person addressed referred to his watch, and answered—'NINE O'CLOCK!'

6

THE TRAVELLER'S STORY OF A TERRIBLY STRANGE BED

Shortly after my education at college was finished, I happened to be staying at Paris with an English friend. We were both young men then, and lived, I am afraid, rather a wild life, in the delightful city of our sojourn. One night we were idling about the neighbourhood of the Palais Royal, doubtful to what amusement we should next betake ourselves. My friend proposed a visit to Frascati's; but his suggestion was not to my taste. I knew Frascati's, as the French saying is, by heart; had lost and won plenty of five-franc pieces there, merely for amusement's sake, until it was amusement no longer, and was thoroughly tired, in fact, of all the ghastly respectabilities of such a social anomaly as a respectable gambling house. 'For Heaven's sake,' said I to my friend, 'let us go somewhere where we can see a little genuine, blackguard, poverty-stricken gaming with no false gingerbread glitter thrown over it all. Let us get away from fashionable Frascati's, to a house where they don't mind letting in a man with a ragged coat, or a man with no coat, ragged or otherwise.' 'Very well,' said my friend, 'we needn't go out of the Palais Royal to find the sort of company you want. Here's the place just before us; as blackguard a place, by all report, as you could possibly wish to see.' In another minute we arrived at the door and entered the house.

When we got upstairs, and had left our hats and sticks with the doorkeeper, we were admitted into the chief gambling room. We did not find many people assembled there. But, few as the men were who looked up at us on our entrance, they were all types—lamentably true types—of their respective classes.

We had come to see blackguards; but these men were something worse. There is a comic side, more or less appreciable, in all blackguardism—here there was nothing but tragedy—mute, weird tragedy. The quiet in the room was horrible. The thin, haggard, long-haired young man, whose sunken eyes fiercely watched the turning up of the cards, never spoke; the flabby, fat-faced, pimply player, who pricked his piece of pasteboard perseveringly, to register how often black won, and how often red—never spoke; the dirty, wrinkled old man, with the vulture eyes and the darned greatcoat, who had lost his last sou, and still looked on desperately, after he could play no longer—never spoke. Even the voice of the croupier sounded as if it were strangely dulled and thickened in the atmosphere of the room. I had entered the place to laugh, but the spectacle before me was something to weep over. I soon found it necessary to take refuge in excitement from the depression of spirits which was fast stealing on me. Unfortunately I sought the nearest excitement, by going to the table and beginning to play. Still more unfortunately, as the event will show, I won—won prodigiously; won incredibly; won at such a rate that the regular players at the table crowded round me; and staring at my stakes with hungry, superstitious eyes, whispered to one another that the English stranger was going to break the bank.

The game was Rouge et Noir. I had played at it in every city in Europe, without, however, the care or the wish to study the

Theory of Chances—that philosopher's stone of all gamblers! And a gambler, in the strict sense of the word, I had never been. I was heart-whole from the corroding passion for play. My gaming was a mere idle amusement. I never resorted to it by necessity, because I never knew what it was to want money. I never practised it so incessantly as to lose more than I could afford, or to gain more than I could coolly pocket without being thrown off my balance by my good luck. In short, I had hitherto frequented gambling tables—just as I frequented ball rooms and opera-houses—because they amused me, and because I had nothing better to do with my leisure hours.

But on this occasion it was very different—now, for the first time in my life, I felt what the passion for play really was. My success first bewildered, and then, in the most literal meaning of the word, intoxicated me. Incredible as it may appear, it is nevertheless true that I only lost when I attempted to estimate chances, and played according to previous calculation. If I left everything to luck, and staked without any care or consideration, I was sure to win—to win in the face of every recognized probability in favour of the bank. At first some of the men present ventured their money safely enough on my colour; but I speedily increased my stakes to sums which they dared not risk. One after another they left off playing, and breathlessly looked on at my game.

Still, time after time, I staked higher and higher, and still won. The excitement in the room rose to fever pitch. The silence was interrupted by a deep-muttered chorus of oaths and exclamations in different languages, every time the gold was shovelled across to my side of the table—even the imperturbable croupier dashed his rake on the floor in a (French) fury of astonishment at my success. But one man present preserved his self-possession, and that man was my friend. He came to my side, and whispering in English, begged me to leave the place, satisfied with what I had already gained. I must do him the justice to say that he repeated his warnings and entreaties several times, and only left me and went away after I had rejected his advice (I was to all intents and purposes gambling drunk) in terms which rendered it impossible for him to address me again that night.

Shortly after he had gone, a hoarse voice behind me cried, 'Permit me, my dear sir—permit me to restore to their proper place two napoleons which you have dropped. Wonderful luck, sir! I pledge you my word of honour, as an old soldier, in the course of my long experience in this sort of thing, I never saw such luck as yours—never! Go on, sir—Sacre mille bombes! Go on boldly, and break the bank!'

I turned round and saw, nodding and smiling at me with inveterate civility, a tall man, dressed in a frogged and braided surtout.

If I had been in my senses, I should have considered him, personally, as being rather a suspicious specimen of an old soldier. He had goggling bloodshot eyes, mangy moustaches, and a broken nose. His voice betrayed a barrack-room intonation of the worst order, and he had the dirtiest pair of hands I ever saw—even in France. These little personal peculiarities exercised, however, no repelling influence on me. In the mad excitement, the reckless triumph of that moment, I was ready to 'fraternize' with anybody who encouraged me in my game. I accepted the old soldier's offered pinch of snuff; clapped him on the back, and swore he was the honestest fellow in the world—the most glorious relic of the Grand Army that I had ever met with. 'Go on!' cried my military friend, snapping his fingers in ecstasy—'Go on, and win! Break the bank—Mille tonnerres! my gallant English comrade, break the bank!'

And I *did* go on—went on at such a rate that in another quarter of an hour the croupier called out, 'Gentlemen, the bank has discontinued for tonight.' All the notes, and all the gold in that 'bank', now lay in a heap under my hands; the whole floating capital of the gambling house was waiting to pour into my pockets!

'Tie up the money in your pocket handkerchief, my worthy sir,' said the old soldier, as I wildly plunged my hands into my heap of gold. 'Tie it up, as we used to tie up a bit of dinner in the Grand Army; your winnings are too heavy for any breeches pockets that ever were sewed. There! that's it—shovel them in, notes and all! Credie! what luck! Stop! another napoleon on the floor! Ah! sacre petit polisson de Napoleon! have I found thee at last? Now then, sir—two tight double knots each way with your honourable permission, and the money's safe. Feel it! feel it, fortunate sir! hard and round as a cannonball—Ah, bah! if they had only fired such cannonballs at us at Austerlitz—nom d'une pipe! if they only had! And now, as an ancient grenadier, as an ex-brave of the French army, what remains for me to do? I ask what? Simply this: to entreat my valued English friend to drink a bottle of champagne with me, and toast the goddess Fortune in foaming goblets before we part!'

Excellent ex-brave! Convivial ancient grenadier! Champagne by all means! An English cheer for an old soldier! Hurrah! hurrah! Another English cheer for the goddess Fortune! Hurrah! hurrah! hurrah!

'Bravo! the Englishman; the amiable, gracious Englishman, in whose veins circulates the vivacious blood of France! Another glass? Ah, bah!—the bottle is empty! Never mind! Vive le vin! I, the old soldier, order another bottle, and half a pound of bonbons with it!'

'No, no, ex-brave; never—ancient grenadier! *Your* bottle last time; *my* bottle this. Behold it! Toast away! The French Army! the great Napoleon! the present company! the croupier! the honest croupier's wife and daughters—if he has any! the Ladies generally! everybody in the world!'

By the time the second bottle of champagne was emptied, I felt as if I had been drinking liquid fire—my brain seemed all aflame. No excess in wine had ever had this effect on me before in my life. Was it the result of a stimulant acting upon my system when I was in a highly excited state? Was my stomach in a particularly disordered condition? Or was the champagne amazingly strong?

'Ex-brave of the French Army!' cried I, in a mad state of exhilaration, '*I* am on fire! how are *you*? You have set me on fire. Do you hear, my hero of Austerlitz? Let us have a third bottle of champagne to put the flame out!'

The old soldier wagged his head, rolled his goggle-eyes, until I expected to see them slip out of their sockets; placed his dirty forefinger by the side of his broken nose; solemnly ejaculated 'Coffee!' and immediately ran off into an inner room.

The word pronounced by the eccentric veteran seemed to have a magical effect on the rest of the company present. With one accord they all rose to depart. Probably they had expected to profit by my intoxication; but finding that my new friend was benevolently bent on preventing me from getting dead drunk, had now abandoned all hope of thriving pleasantly on my winnings. Whatever their motive might be, at any rate they went away in a body. When the old soldier returned, and sat down again opposite to me at the table, we had the room to ourselves. I could see the croupier, in a sort of vestibule which opened out of it, eating his supper in solitude. The silence was now deeper than ever.

A sudden change, too, had come over the 'ex-brave'. He assumed a portentously solemn look; and when he spoke to me again, his speech was ornamented by no oaths, enforced by no finger-snapping, enlivened by no apostrophes or exclamations.

'Listen, my dear sir,' said he, in mysteriously confidential tones—'listen to an old soldier's advice. I have been to the mistress of the house (a very charming woman, with a genius for cookery!) to impress on her the necessity of making us some particularly strong and good coffee. You must drink this coffee in order to get rid of your little amiable exaltation of spirits before you think of going home—you *must*, my good and gracious friend! With all that money to take home tonight, it is a sacred duty to yourself to have your wits about you. You are known to be a winner to an enormous extent by several gentlemen present tonight, who, in a certain point of view, are very worthy and excellent fellows; but they are mortal men, my dear sir, and they have their amiable weaknesses. Need I say more? Ah, no, no! you understand me! Now, this is what you must do—send for a cabriolet when you feel quite well again—draw up all the windows when you get into it—and tell the driver to take you home only through the large and well-lighted thoroughfares. Do this; and you and your money will be safe. Do this; and tomorrow you will thank an old soldier for giving you a word of honest advice.'

Just as the ex-brave ended his oration in very lachrymose tones, the coffee came in, ready poured out in two cups. My attentive friend handed me one of the cups with a bow. I was parched with thirst, and drank it off at a draught. Almost instantly afterwards, I was seized with a fit of giddiness, and felt more completely intoxicated than ever. The room whirled round and round furiously; the old soldier seemed to be regularly bobbing up and down before me like the piston of a steam-engine. I was half deafened by a violent singing in my ears; a feeling of utter bewilderment, helplessness, idiocy, overcame me. I rose from my chair, holding on by the table to keep my balance; and stammered out that I felt dreadfully unwell—so unwell that I did not know how I was to get home.

'My dear friend,' answered the old soldier—and even his

voice seemed to be bobbing up and down as he spoke—'my dear friend, it would be madness to go home in *your* state; you would be sure to lose your money; you might be robbed and murdered with the greatest ease. *I* am going to sleep here; do *you* sleep here, too—they make up capital beds in this house—take one; sleep off the effects of the wine, and go home safely with your winnings tomorrow—tomorrow, in broad daylight.'

I had but two ideas left: one, that I must never let go hold of my handkerchief full of money; the other, that I must lie down somewhere immediately, and fall off into a comfortable sleep. So I agreed to the proposal about the bed, and took the offered arm of the old soldier, carrying my money with my disengaged hand. Preceded by the croupier, we passed along some passages and up a flight of stairs into the bedroom which I was to occupy. The ex-brave shook me warmly by the hand, proposed that we should breakfast together, and then, followed by the croupier, left me for the night.

I ran to the wash-hand stand; drank some of the water in my jug; poured the rest out, and plunged my face into it; then sat down in a chair and tried to compose myself. I soon felt better. The change for my lungs, from the fetid atmosphere of the gambling room to the cool air of the apartment I now occupied, the almost equally refreshing change for my eyes, from the glaring gaslights of the 'salon' to the dim, quiet flicker of one bedroom candle, aided wonderfully the restorative effects of cold water. The giddiness left me, and I began to feel a little like a reasonable being again. My first thought was of the risk of sleeping all night in a gambling house; my second, of the still greater risk of trying to get out after the house was closed, and of going home alone at night through the streets of Paris with a large sum of money about me. I had slept in worse places than this on my travels; so I determined to lock, bolt, and barricade my door, and take my chance till the next morning.

Accordingly, I secured myself against all intrusion; looked under the bed, and into the cupboard; tried the fastening of the window; and then, satisfied that I had taken every proper precaution, pulled off my upper clothing, put my light, which was a dim one, on the hearth among a feathery litter of wood-ashes, and got into bed, with the handkerchief full of money under my pillow.

I soon felt not only that I could not go to sleep, but that I could not even close my eyes. I was wide awake, and in a high fever. Every nerve in my body trembled—every one of my senses seemed to be preternaturally sharpened. I tossed and rolled, and tried every kind of position, and perseveringly sought out the cold corners of the bed, and all to no purpose. Now I thrust my arms over the clothes; now I poked them under the clothes; now I violently shot my legs straight out down to the bottom of the bed; now I convulsively coiled them up as near my chin as they would go; now I shook out my crumpled pillow, changed it to the cool side, patted it flat, and lay down quietly on my back; now I fiercely doubled it in two, set it up on end, thrust it against the board of the bed, and tried a sitting posture. Every effort was in vain; I groaned with vexation as I felt that I was in for a sleepless night.

What could I do? I had no book to read. And yet, unless I found out some method of diverting my mind, I felt certain that I was in the condition to imagine all sorts of horrors; to rack my brain with forebodings of every possible and impossible danger; in short, to pass the night in suffering all conceivable varieties of nervous terror.

I raised myself on my elbow, and looked about the room—which was brightened by a lovely moonlight pouring straight through the window—to see if it contained any pictures or ornaments that I could at all clearly distinguish. While my eyes wandered from wall to wall, a remembrance of Le Maistre's delightful little book, *Voyage autour de ma Chambre*, occurred to me. I resolved to imitate the French author, and find occupation and amusement enough to relieve the tedium of my wakefulness, by making a mental inventory of every article of furniture I could see, and by following up to their sources the multitude of associations which even a chair, a table, or a wash-hand stand may be made to call forth.

In the nervous unsettled state of my mind at that moment, I found it much easier to make my inventory than to make my reflections, and thereupon soon gave up all hope of thinking in Le Maistre's fanciful track—or, indeed, of thinking at all. I looked about the room at the different articles of furniture, and did nothing more.

There was, first, the bed I was lying in; a four-post bed, of all things in the world to meet with in Paris—yes, a thorough clumsy British four-poster, with the regular top lined with chintz—the regular fringed valance all round—the regular stifling, unwholesome curtains, which I remembered having mechanically drawn back against the posts without particularly noticing the bed when I first got into the room. Then there was the marble-topped wash-hand stand, from which the water I had spilled, in my hurry to pour it out, was still dripping, slowly and more slowly, on to the brick floor. Then two small chairs, with my coat, waistcoat, and trousers flung on them. Then a large elbow-chair covered with dirty-white dimity, with my cravat and shirt collar thrown over the back. Then a chest of drawers with two of the brass handles off, and a tawdry, broken china inkstand placed on it by way of ornament for the top. Then the dressing-table, adorned by a very small looking-glass, and a very large pincushion. Then the window—an unusually large window. Then a dark old picture, which the feeble candle dimly showed me. It was a picture of a fellow in a high Spanish hat, crowned with a plume of towering feathers. A swarthy, sinister ruffian, looking upward, shading his eyes with his hand, and looking intently upward—it might be at some tall gallows at which he was going to be hanged. At any rate, he had the appearance of thoroughly deserving it.

This picture put a kind of constraint upon me to look upward too—at the top of the bed. It was a gloomy and not an interesting object, and I looked back at the picture. I counted the feathers in the man's hat—they stood out in relief—three white, two green. I observed the crown of his hat, which was of conical shape, according to the fashion supposed to have been favoured by Guido Fawkes. I wondered what he was looking up at. It couldn't be at the stars; such a desperado was neither astrologer nor astronomer. It must be at the high gallows, and he was going to be hanged presently. Would the executioner come into possession of his conical crowned hat and plume of feathers? I counted the feathers again—three white, two green.

While I still lingered over this very improving and intellectual employment, my thoughts insensibly began to wander. The moonlight shining into the room reminded me of a certain moonlight night in England—the night after a picnic party in a Welsh valley. Every incident of the drive homeward, through lovely scenery, which the moonlight made lovelier than ever, came back to my remembrance, though I had never given the picnic a thought for years; though, if I had *tried* to recollect it, I could certainly have recalled little or nothing of that scene long past. Of all the wonderful faculties that help to tell us we are immortal, which speaks the sublime truth more eloquently than memory? Here was I, in a strange house of the most suspicious character, in a situation of uncertainty, and even of peril, which might seem to make the cool exercise of my recollection almost out of the question; nevertheless, remembering, quite involuntarily, places, people, conversations, minute circumstances of every kind, which

I had thought forgotten for ever; which I could not possibly have recalled at will, even under the most favourable auspices. And what cause had produced in a moment the whole of this strange, complicated, mysterious effect? Nothing but some rays of moonlight shining in at my bedroom window.

I was still thinking of the picnic—of our merriment on the drive home—of the sentimental young lady who *would* quote 'Childe Harold' because it was moonlight. I was absorbed by these past scenes and past amusements, when, in an instant, the thread on which my memories hung snapped asunder; my attention immediately came back to present things more vividly than ever, and I found myself, I neither knew why nor wherefore, looking hard at the picture again.

Looking for what?

Good God! the man had pulled his hat down on his brows! No! the hat itself was gone! Where was the conical crown? Where the feathers—three white, two green? Not there! In place of the hat and feathers, what dusky object was it that now hid his forehead, his eyes, his shading hand?

Was the bed moving?

I turned on my back and looked up. Was I mad? drunk? dreaming? giddy again? or was the top of the bed really moving down—sinking slowly, regularly, silently, horribly, right down throughout the whole of its length and breadth—right down upon me, as I lay underneath?

My blood seemed to stand still. A deadly paralysing coldness stole all over me as I turned my head round on the pillow and determined to test whether the bed-top was really moving or not, by keeping my eye on the man in the picture.

The next look in that direction was enough. The dull, black, frowzy outline of the valance above me was within an inch of being parallel with his waist. I still looked breathlessly. And steadily and slowly—very slowly—I saw the figure, and the line of frame below the figure, vanish, as the valance moved down before it.

I am, constitutionally, anything but timid. I have been on more than one occasion in peril of my life, and have not lost my self-possession for an instant; but when the conviction first settled on my mind that the bed-top was really moving, was steadily and continuously sinking down upon me, I looked up shuddering, helpless, panic-stricken, beneath the hideous machinery for murder, which was advancing closer and closer to suffocate me where I lay.

I looked up, motionless, speechless, breathless. The candle, fully spent, went out; but the moonlight still brightened the room. Down and down, without pausing and without sounding, came the bed-top, and still my panic-terror seemed to bind me faster and faster to the mattress on which I lay—down and down it sank, till the dusty odour from the lining of the canopy came stealing into my nostrils.

At that final moment the instinct of self-preservation startled me out of my trance, and I moved at last. There was just room for me to roll myself sidewise off the bed. As I dropped noiselessly to the floor, the edge of the murderous canopy touched me on the shoulder.

Without stopping to draw my breath, without wiping the cold sweat from my face, I rose instantly on my knees to watch the bed-top. I was literally spellbound by it. If I had heard footsteps behind me, I could not have turned round; if a means of escape had been miraculously provided for me, I could not have moved to take advantage of it. The whole life in me was, at that moment, concentrated in my eyes.

It descended—the whole canopy, with the fringe round it, came down—down—close down; so close that there was not room now to squeeze my finger between the bed-top and the bed. I felt at the sides, and discovered that what had appeared to me from beneath to be the ordinary light canopy of a four-post bed was in reality a thick, broad mattress, the substance of which was concealed by the valance and its fringe. I looked up and saw the four posts rising hideously bare. In the middle of the bed-top was a huge wooden screw that had evidently worked it down through a hole in the ceiling, just as ordinary presses are worked down on the substance selected for compression. The frightful apparatus moved without making the faintest noise. There had been no creaking as it came down; there was now not the faintest sound from the room above. Amid a dead and awful silence I beheld before me—in the nineteenth century, and in the civilized capital of France—such a machine for secret murder by suffocation as might have existed in the worst days of the Inquisition, in the lonely inns among the Hartz Mountains, in the mysterious tribunals of Westphalia! Still, as I looked on it, I could not move, I could hardly breathe, but I began to recover the power of thinking, and in a moment I discovered the murderous conspiracy framed against me in all its horror.

My cup of coffee had been drugged, and drugged too strongly. I had been saved from being smothered by having taken an overdose of some narcotic. How I had chafed and fretted at the fever-fit which had preserved my life by keeping me awake! How recklessly I had confided myself to the two wretches who had led me into this room, determined, for the sake of my winnings, to kill me in my sleep by the surest and most horrible contrivance for secretly accomplishing my destruction! How many men, winners like me, had slept, as I had proposed to sleep, in that bed, and had never been seen or heard of more! I shuddered at the bare idea of it.

But, ere long, all thought was again suspended by the sight of the murderous canopy moving once more. After it had remained on the bed—as nearly as I could guess—about ten minutes, it began to move up again. The villains who worked it from above evidently believed that their purpose was now accomplished. Slowly and silently, as it had descended, that horrible bed-top rose towards its former place. When it reached the upper extremities of the four posts, it reached the ceiling, too. Neither hole nor screw could be seen; the bed became in appearance an ordinary bed again—the canopy an ordinary canopy—even to the most suspicious eyes.

Now, for the first time, I was able to move—to rise from my knees—to dress myself in my upper clothing—and to consider of how I should escape. If I betrayed by the smallest noise that the attempt to suffocate me had failed, I was certain to be murdered. Had I made any noise already? I listened intently, looking towards the door.

No! no footsteps in the passage outside—no sound of a tread, light or heavy, in the room above—absolute silence everywhere. Besides locking and bolting my door, I had moved an old wooden chest against it, which I had found under the bed. To remove this chest (my blood ran cold as I thought of what its contents *might* be!) without making some disturbance was impossible; and, moreover, to think of escaping through the house, now barred up for the night, was sheer insanity. Only one chance was left me—the window. I stole to it on tiptoe.

My bedroom was on the first floor, above an entresol, and looked into a back street. I raised my hand to open the window, knowing that on that action hung, by the merest hair's breadth, my chance of safety. They keep vigilant watch in a House of Murder. If any part of the frame cracked, if the hinge creaked, I was a lost man! It must have occupied me at least five minutes, reckoning by time—five *hours*, reckoning by suspense—to open that window. I succeeded in doing it silently—in doing it with all the dexterity of a housebreaker—and then looked down into the street. To leap the distance beneath me would be almost certain destruction! Next, I looked round at the sides of the house. Down the left side ran a thick water-pipe—it passed close by the outer edge of the window. The moment I saw the pipe I knew I was saved. My breath came and went freely for the first time since I had seen the canopy of the bed moving down upon me!

To some men the means of escape which I had discovered might have seemed difficult and dangerous enough—to *me* the prospect of slipping down the pipe into the street did not suggest even a thought of peril. I had always been accustomed, by the practice of gymnastics, to keep up my schoolboy powers as a daring and expert climber; and knew that my head, hands, and feet would serve me faithfully in any hazards of ascent or descent. I had already got one leg over the windowsill, when I remembered the handkerchief filled with money under my pillow. I could well have afforded to leave it behind me, but I was revengefully determined that the miscreants of the gambling house should miss their plunder as well as their victim. So I went back to the bed and tied the heavy handkerchief at my back by my cravat.

Just as I had made it tight and fixed it in a comfortable place, I thought I heard a sound of breathing outside the door. The chill feeling of horror ran through me again as I listened. No! dead silence still in the passage—I had only heard the night air blowing softly into the room. The next moment I was on the windowsill—and the next I had a firm grip on the water-pipe with my hands and knees.

I slid down into the street easily and quietly, as I thought I should, and immediately set off at the top of my speed to a branch 'Prefecture' of Police, which I knew was situated in the immediate neighbourhood. A 'Sub-prefect', and several picked men among his subordinates, happened to be up, maturing, I believe, some scheme for discovering the perpetrator of a mysterious murder which all Paris was talking of just then.

When I began my story, in a breathless hurry and in very bad French, I could see that the Sub-prefect suspected me of being a drunken Englishman who had robbed somebody; but he soon altered his opinion as I went on, and before I had anything like concluded, he shoved all the papers before him into a drawer, put on his hat, supplied me with another (for I was bareheaded), ordered a file of soldiers, desired his expert followers to get ready all sorts of tools for breaking open doors and ripping up brick flooring, and took my arm, in the most friendly and familiar manner possible, to lead me with him out of the house. I will venture to say that when the Sub-prefect was a little boy, and was taken for the first time to the play, he was not half as much pleased as he was now at the job in prospect for him at the gambling house!

Away we went through the streets, the Sub-prefect cross-examining and congratulating me in the same breath as we marched at the head of our formidable posse comitatus. Sentinels were placed at the back and front of the house the moment we got to it; a tremendous battery of knocks was directed against the door; a light appeared at a window; I was told to conceal myself behind the police—then came more knocks and a cry of 'Open in the name of the law!' At that terrible summons bolts and locks gave way before an invisible hand, and the moment after the Sub-prefect was in the passage, confronting a waiter half-dressed and ghastly pale. This was the short dialogue which immediately took place:

'We want to see the Englishman who is sleeping in this house?'

'He went away hours ago.'

'He did no such thing. His friend went away; *he* remained. Show us to his bedroom!'

'I swear to you, Monsieur le Sous-prefect, he is not here! he—'

'I swear to you, Monsieur le Garcon, he is. He slept here—he didn't find your bed comfortable—he came to us to complain of it—here he is among my men—and here am I ready to look for a flea or two in his bedstead. Renaudin! (calling to one of the subordinates, and pointing to the waiter) collar that man and tie his hands behind him. Now, then, gentlemen, let us walk upstairs!'

Every man and woman in the house was secured—the 'Old Soldier' the first. Then I identified the bed in which I had slept, and then we went into the room above.

No object that was at all extraordinary appeared in any part of it. The Sub-prefect looked round the place, commanded everybody to be silent, stamped twice on the floor, called for a candle, looked attentively at the spot he had stamped on, and ordered the flooring there to be carefully taken up. This was done in no time. Lights were produced, and we saw a deep raftered cavity between the floor of this room and the ceiling of the room beneath. Through this cavity there ran perpendicularly a sort of case of iron thickly greased; and inside the case appeared the screw, which communicated with the bed-top below. Extra lengths of screw, freshly oiled; levers covered with felt; all the complete upper works of a heavy press—constructed with infernal ingenuity so as to join the fixtures below, and when taken to pieces again, to go into the smallest possible compass—were next discovered and pulled out on the floor. After some little difficulty the Sub-prefect succeeded in putting the machinery together, and, leaving his men to work it, descended with me to the bedroom. The smothering canopy was then lowered, but not so noiselessly as I had seen it lowered. When I mentioned this to the Sub-prefect, his answer, simple as it was, had a terrible significance. 'My men,' said he, 'are working down the bed-top for the first time—the men whose money you won were in better practice.'

We left the house in the sole possession of two police agents—every one of the inmates being removed to prison on the spot. The Sub-prefect, after taking down my proces verbal in his office, returned with me to my hotel to get my passport. 'Do you think,' I asked, as I gave it to him, 'that any men have really been smothered in that bed, as they tried to smother *me*?'

'I have seen dozens of drowned men laid out at the Morgue,' answered the Sub-prefect, 'in whose pocketbooks were found letters stating that they had committed suicide in the Seine, because they had lost everything at the gaming table. Do I know how many of those men entered the same gambling house that *you* entered? won as *you* won? took that bed as *you* took it? slept in it? were smothered in it? and were privately thrown into the river, with a letter of explanation written by the murderers and placed in their pocketbooks? No man can say how many or how few have suffered the fate from which you have escaped. The people of the gambling house kept their bedstead machinery a secret from *us*—even from the police! The dead kept the rest of the secret for them. Good-night, or rather good morning, Monsieur Faulkner! Be at my office again at nine o'clock—in the meantime, au revoir!'

The rest of my story is soon told. I was examined and re-examined; the gambling house was strictly searched all through from top to bottom; the prisoners were separately interrogated; and two of the less guilty among them made a confession. I discovered that the Old Soldier was the master of the gambling house—*justice* discovered that he had been drummed out of the army as a vagabond years ago; that he had been guilty of all sorts of villainies since; that he was in possession of stolen property, which the owners identified; and that he, the croupier, another accomplice, and the woman who had made my cup of coffee, were all in the secret of the bedstead. There appeared some reason to doubt whether the inferior persons attached to the house knew anything of the suffocating machinery; and they received the benefit of that doubt, by being treated simply as thieves and vagabonds. As for the Old Soldier and his two head myrmidons, they went to the galleys; the woman who had drugged my coffee was imprisoned for I forget how many years; the regular attendants at the gambling house were considered 'suspicious' and placed under 'surveillance'; and I became, for one whole week (which is a long time) the head 'lion' in Parisian society. My adventure was dramatized by three illustrious playmakers, but never saw theatrical daylight; for the censorship forbade the introduction on the stage of a correct copy of the gambling house bedstead.

One good result was produced by my adventure, which any censorship must have approved: it cured me of ever again trying *Rouge et Noir* as an amusement. The sight of a green cloth, with packs of cards and heaps of money on it, will henceforth be for ever associated in my mind with the sight of a bed canopy descending to suffocate me in the silence and darkness of the night.

7

THE TWIN SISTERS: A TRUE STORY

Among those who attended the first of the King's levées, during the London season of 18—, was an unmarried gentleman of large fortune, named Streatfield. While his carriage was proceeding slowly down St. James's Street, he naturally sought such amusement and occupation as he could find in looking on the brilliant scene around him. The day was unusually fine; crowds of spectators thronged the street and the balconies of the houses on either side of it, all gazing at the different equipages with as eager a curiosity and interest, as if fine vehicles and fine people inside them were the rarest objects of contemplation in the whole metropolis. Proceeding at a slower and slower pace, Mr Streatfield's carriage had just arrived at the middle of the street, when a longer stoppage than usual occurred. He looked carelessly up at the nearest balcony; and there, among some eight or ten ladies, all strangers to him, he saw one face that riveted his attention immediately.

He had never beheld anything so beautiful, anything which struck him with such strange, mingled, and sudden sensations, as this face. He gazed and gazed on it, hardly knowing where he was, or what he was doing, until the line of vehicles began again to move on. Then—after first ascertaining the number of the house—he flung himself back in the carriage, and tried to examine his feelings, to reason himself into self-possession; but it was all in vain. He was seized with that amiable form of social monomania, called 'love at first sight'.

He entered the palace, greeted his friends, and performed all the necessary Court ceremonies, feeling the whole time like a man in a trance. He spoke mechanically, and moved mechanically—the lovely face in the balcony occupied his thoughts to the exclusion of everything else. On his return home, he had engagements for the afternoon and evening—he forgot and broke them all; and walked back to St. James's Street as soon as he had changed his dress.

The balcony was empty; the sightseers who had filled it but a few hours before, had departed—but obstacles of all sorts now tended only to stimulate Mr Streatfield; he was determined to ascertain the parentage of the young lady, determined to look on the lovely face again—the thermometer of his heart had risen already to Fever Heat! Without loss of time, the shopkeeper to whom the house belonged was bribed to loquacity by a purchase. All that he could tell, in answer to inquiries, was that he had let his lodgings to an elderly gentleman and his wife, from the country, who had asked some friends into their balcony to see the carriages go to the levée. Nothing daunted, Mr Streatfield questioned and questioned again. What was the old gentleman's name?—Dimsdale—Could he see Mr Dimsdale's servant?—The obsequious shopkeeper had no doubt that he could: Mr Dimsdale's servant should be sent for immediately.

In a few minutes the servant, the all-important link in the chain of Love's evidence, made his appearance. He was a pompous, portly man, who listened with solemn attention, with a stern judicial calmness, to Mr Streatfield's rapid and somewhat confused inquiries, which were accompanied by a minute description of the young lady, and by several explanatory statements, all very fictitious, and all very plausible. Stupid as the servant was, and suspicious as all stupid people are, he had nevertheless sense enough to perceive that he was addressed by a gentleman, and gratitude enough to feel considerably mollified by the handsome douceur which was quietly slipped into his hand. After much pondering and doubting, he at last arrived at the conclusion that the fair object of Mr Streatfield's inquiries was a Miss Langley, who joined the party in the balcony that morning, with her sister; and who was the daughter of Mr Langley, of Langley Hall, in —shire. The family were now staying in London, at — Street. More information than this, the servant stated that he could not afford—he was certain that he had made no mistake, for the Miss Langleys were the only very young ladies in the house that morning—however, if Mr Streatfield wished to speak to his master, he was ready to carry any message with which he might be charged.

But Mr Streatfield had already heard enough for his purpose, and departed at once for his club, determined to discover some means of being introduced in due form to Miss Langley, before he slept that night—though he should travel round the whole circle of his acquaintance—high and low, rich and poor—on making the attempt. Arrived at the club, he began to inquire resolutely, in all directions, for a friend who knew Mr Langley, of Langley Hall. He disturbed gastronomic gentlemen at their dinner; he interrupted agricultural gentlemen who were deep in the moaning over the prospects of the harvest; he startled literary gentlemen who were deep in the critical mysteries of the last Review; he invaded billiard-room, dressing-room, smoking room; he was more like a frantic ministerial whipper-in, hunting up stray members for a division than an ordinary man; and the oftener he was defeated in his object, the more determined he was to succeed. At last, just as he had vainly inquired of everybody that he knew, just as he was standing in the hall of the clubhouse thinking where he should go next, a friend entered, who at once relieved him of all his difficulties—a precious, an inestimable man, who was on intimate terms with Mr Langley, and had been lately staying at Langley Hall. To this friend all the lover's cares and anxieties were at once confided; and a fitter depositary for such secrets of the heart could hardly have been found. He made no jokes—for he was not a bachelor; he abstained from shaking his head and recommending prudence—for he was not a seasoned husband, or an experienced widower; what he really did was to enter heart and soul into his friend's projects—for he was precisely in that position, the only position, in which the male sex generally take a proper interest in matchmaking: he was a newly married man.

Two days after, Mr Streatfield was the happiest of mortals—he was introduced to the lady of his love, to Miss Jane Langley. He really enjoyed the priceless privilege of looking once more on the face in the balcony, and looking on it almost as often as he wished. It was perfect Elysium. Mr and Mrs Langley saw little, or no company—Miss Jane was always accessible, never monopolized—the light of her beauty shone, day after day, for her adorer alone; and his love blossomed in it, fast as flowers in a hothouse. Passing quickly by all the minor details of the wooing to arrive the sooner at the grand fact of the winning, let us simply relate that Mr Streatfield's object in seeking an introduction to Mr Langley was soon explained, and was indeed visible enough long before the explanation. He was a handsome man, an accomplished man, and a rich man. His first two qualifications conquered the daughter, and his third the father. In six weeks Mr Streatfield was the accepted suitor of Miss Jane Langley.

The wedding day was fixed—it was arranged that the marriage should take place at Langley Hall, whither the family proceeded, leaving the unwilling lover in London, a prey to all the inexorable business formalities of the occasion. For ten days did the ruthless lawyers—those dead weights that burden the back of Hymen—keep their victim imprisoned in the metropolis, occupied over settlements that never seemed likely to be settled. But even the long march of the Law has its end like other mortal things: at the expiration of the ten days all was completed, and Mr Streatfield found himself at liberty to start for Langley Hall.

A large party was assembled at the house to grace the approaching nuptials. There were to be tableaux, charades, boating trips, riding excursions, amusements of all sorts—the whole to conclude (in the playbill phrase) with the grand climax of the wedding. Mr Streatfield arrived late; dinner was ready; he had barely time to dress, and then the bustle into the drawing room, just as the guests were leaving it, to offer his arm to Miss Jane—all greetings with friends and introductions to strangers being postponed till the party met round the dining table.

Grace had been said; the covers were taken off; the loud cheerful hum of conversation was just beginning, when Mr Streatfield's eyes met the eyes of a young lady who was seated opposite, at the table. The guests near him, observing at the same moment, that he continued standing after every one else had been placed, glanced at him inquiringly. To their astonishment and alarm, they observed that his face had suddenly become deadly pale—his rigid features looked struck in paralysis. Several of his friends spoke to him; but for the first few moments he returned no answer. Then, still fixing his eyes upon the young lady opposite, he abruptly exclaimed in a voice, the altered tones of which startled every one who heard him, '*That* is the face I saw in the balcony!—*that* woman is the only woman I can ever marry!' The next instant, without a word more either of explanation or apology, he hurried from the room.

One or two of the guests mechanically started up, as if to follow him; the rest remained at the table, looking on each other in speechless surprise. But, before any one could either act or speak, almost at the moment when the door closed on Mr Streatfield, the attention of all was painfully directed to Jane Langley. She had fainted. Her mother and sisters removed her from the room immediately, aided by the servants. As they disappeared, a dead silence again sank down over the company—they all looked round with one accord to the master of the house.

Mr Langley's face and manner sufficiently revealed the suffering and suspense that he was secretly enduring. But he was a man of the world—neither by word nor action did he betray what was passing within him. He resumed his place at the table, and begged his guests to do the same. He affected to make light of what had happened; entreated every one to forget it, or, if they remembered it at all, to remember it only as a mere accident which would no doubt be satisfactorily explained. Perhaps it was only a jest on Mr Streatfield's part—rather too serious a one, he must own. At any rate, whatever was the cause of the interruption to the dinner which had just happened, it was not important enough to require everybody to fast around the table of the feast. He asked it as a favour to himself that no further notice might be taken of what had occurred. While Mr Langley was speaking thus, he hastily wrote a few lines on a piece of paper, and gave it to one of the servants. The note was directed to Mr Streatfield; the lines contained only these words: 'Two hours hence, I shall expect to see you alone in the library.'

The dinner proceeded; the places occupied by the female members of the Langley family, and by the young lady who had attracted Mr Streatfield's notice in so extraordinary a manner, being left vacant. Every one present endeavoured to follow Mr

Langley's advice, and go through the business of the dinner, as if nothing had occurred; but the attempt failed miserably. Long, blank pauses occurred in the conversation; general topics were started, but never pursued; it was more like an assembly of strangers than a meeting of friends; people neither ate nor drank, as they were accustomed to eat and drink; they talked in altered voices, and sat with unusual stillness, even in the same positions. Relatives, friends, and acquaintances, all alike perceived that some great domestic catastrophe had happened; all foreboded that some serious, if not fatal, explanation of Mr Streatfield's conduct would ensue: and it was vain and hopeless—a very mockery of self-possession—to attempt to shake off the sinister and chilling influences that recent events had left behind them, and resume at will the thoughtlessness and hilarity of ordinary life.

Still, however, Mr Langley persisted in doing the honours of his table, in proceeding doggedly through all the festive ceremonies of the hour, until the ladies rose and retired. Then, after looking at his watch, he beckoned to one of his sons to take his place; and quietly left the room. He only stopped once, as he crossed the hall, to ask news of his daughter from one of the servants. The reply was that she had had a hysterical fit; that the medical attendant of the family had been sent for; and that since his arrival she had become more composed. When the man had spoken, Mr Langley made no remark, but proceeded at once to the library. He locked the door behind him, as soon as he entered the room.

Mr Streatfield was already waiting there—he was seated at the table, endeavouring to maintain an appearance of composure, by mechanically turning over the leaves of the books before him. Mr Langley drew a chair near him; and in low, but very firm tones, began the conversation thus:

'I have given you two hours, sir, to collect yourself, to

consider your position fully—I presume, therefore, that you are now prepared to favour me with an explanation of your conduct at my table today.'

'What explanation can I make?—what can I say, or think of this most terrible of fatalities?' exclaimed Mr Streatfield, speaking faintly and confusedly; and still not looking up— 'There has been an unexampled error committed!—a fatal mistake, which I could never have anticipated, and over which I had no control!'

'Enough, sir, of the language of romance,' interrupted Mr Langley, coldly; 'I am neither of an age nor a disposition to appreciate it. I come here to ask plain questions honestly, and I insist, as my right, on receiving answers in the same spirit. *You*, Mr Streatfield, sought an introduction to *me*—you professed attached to my daughter Jane—your proposals were (I fear unhappily for *us*) accepted—your weddingday was fixed—and now, after all this, when you happen to observe my daughter's twin sister sitting opposite to you—'

'Her twin sister!' exclaimed Mr Streatfield; and his trembling hand crumpled the leaves of the book, which he still held while he spoke. 'Why is it, intimate as I have been with your family, that I now know for the first time that Miss Jane Langley has a twin sister?'

'Do you descend, sir, to a subterfuge, when I ask you for an explanation?' returned Mr Langley, angrily. 'You must have heard, over and over again, that my children, Jane and Clara, were twins.'

'On my word and honour, I declare that—'

'Spare me all appeals to your word or your honour, sir; I am beginning to doubt both.'

'I will not make the unhappy situation, in which we are all placed, still worse, by answering your last words, as I might, at other times, feel inclined to answer them,' said Mr Streatfield, assuming a calmer demeanour than he had hitherto displayed. 'I tell you the truth, when I tell you that, before today, I never knew that any of your children were twins. Your daughter, Jane, has frequently spoken to me of her absent sister, Clara, but never spoke of her as her twin sister. Until today, I have had no opportunity of discovering the truth; for until today, I have never met Miss Clara Langley since I saw her in the balcony of the house in St. James's Street. The only one of your children who was never present during my intercourse with your family, in London, was your daughter Clara—the daughter whom I now know, for the first time, as the young lady who really arrested my attention on my way to the levée—whose affections it was really my object to win in seeking an introduction to you. To *me*, the resemblance between the twin sisters has been a fatal resemblance; the long absence of one, a fatal absence.'

There was a momentary pause, as Mr Streatfield sadly and calmly pronounced the last words. Mr Langley appeared to be absorbed in thought. At length he proceeded, speaking to himself:

'It *is* strange! I remember that Clara left London on the day of the levée, to set out on a visit to her aunt; and only returned here two days since, to be present at her sister's marriage. Well, sir,' he continued, addressing Mr Streatfield, 'granting what you say, granting that we all mentioned my absent daughter to you, as we are accustomed to mention her among ourselves, simply as 'Clara', you have still not excused your conduct in my eyes. Remarkable as the resemblance is between the sisters, more remarkable even, I am willing to admit, than the resemblance usually is between twins, there is yet a difference, which slight, indescribable though it may be, is nevertheless discernible to all their relations and to all their friends. How is it that you, who represent yourself as so vividly impressed by your first sight of my daughter Clara, did not discover the error when you were introduced to her sister Jane, as the lady who had so much attracted you?'

'You forget, sir,' rejoined Mr Streatfield, 'that I have never beheld the sisters together until today. Though both were in the balcony when I first looked up at it, it was Miss Clara Langley alone who attracted my attention. Had I only received the smallest hint that the absent sister of Miss Jane Langley was her *twin sister*, I would have seen her, at any sacrifice, before making my proposals. For it is my duty to confess to you, Mr Langley (with the candour which is your undoubted due), that when I was first introduced to your daughter Jane, I felt an unaccountable impression that she was the same as, and yet different from, the lady whom I had seen in the balcony. Soon, however, this impression wore off. Under the circumstances, could I regard it as anything but a mere caprice, a lover's wayward fancy? I dismissed it from my mind; it ceased to affect me, until today, when I first discovered that it was a warning which I had most unhappily disregarded; that a terrible error had been committed, for which no one of us was to blame, but which was fraught with misery, undeserved misery, to us all!'

'These, Mr Streatfield, are explanations which may satisfy *you*,' said Mr Langley, in a milder tone, 'but they cannot satisfy *me*; they will not satisfy the world. You have repudiated, in the most public and most abrupt manner, an engagement, in the fulfilment of which the honour and the happiness of my family are concerned. You have given me reasons for your conduct, it is true; but will those reasons restore to my daughter the tranquillity which she has lost, perhaps for ever? Will they stop the whisperings of calumny? Will they carry conviction to those strangers to me, or enemies of mine, whose pleasure it may be to disbelieve them? You have placed both yourself and me, sir, in a position of embarrassment—nay, a position of danger and disgrace, from which the strongest reasons and the best excuses cannot extricate us.'

'I entreat you to believe,' replied Mr Streatfield, 'that I deplore from my heart the error—the fault, if you will—of which I have been unconsciously guilty. I implore your pardon, both for what I said and did at your table today; but I cannot do more. I cannot and I dare not pronounce the marriage vows to your daughter, with my lips, when I know that neither my conscience nor my heart can ratify them. The commonest justice, and the commonest respect towards a young lady who deserves both, and more than both, from every one who approaches her, strengthen me to persevere in the only course which it is consistent with honour and integrity for me to take.'

'You appear to forget,' said Mr Langley, 'that it is not merely your own honour, but the honour of others, that is to be considered in the course of conduct which you are now to pursue.'

'I have by no means forgotten what is due to *you*,' continued Mr Streatfield, 'or what responsibilities I have incurred from the nature of my intercourse with your family. Do I put too much trust in your forbearance, if I now assure you, candidly and unreservedly, that I still place all my hopes of happiness in the prospect of becoming connected by marriage with a daughter of yours? Miss Clara Langley—'

Here the speaker paused. His position was becoming a delicate and a dangerous one; but he made no effort to withdraw from it. Almost bewildered by the pressing and perilous emergency of the moment, harassed by such a tumult of conflicting emotions within him as he had never known before, he risked the worst, with all the blindfold desperation of love. The angry flush was rising on Mr Langley's cheek; it was evidently costing him a severe struggle to retain his assumed self-possession; but he did not speak. After an interval, Mr Streatfield proceeded thus:

'However unfortunately I may express myself, I am sure you will do me the justice to believe that I am now speaking from my heart on a subject (to *me*) of the most vital importance. Place yourself in my situation, consider all that has happened, consider that this may be, for aught I know to the contrary, the last opportunity I may have of pleading my cause; and then say whether it is possible for me to conceal from you that I can only look to your forbearance and sympathy for permission to retrieve my error, to—to—Mr Langley! I cannot choose expressions at such a moment as this. I can only tell you that the feeling with which I regarded your daughter Clara, when I first saw her, still remains what it was. I cannot analyse it; I cannot reconcile its apparent inconsistencies and contradictions; I cannot explain how, while I may seem to you and to every one to have varied and vacillated with insolent caprice, I have really remained, in my own heart and to my own conscience, true to my first sensations and my first convictions. I can only implore you not to condemn me to a life of disappointment and misery, by judging me with hasty irritation. Favour me, so far at least, as to relate the conversation which has passed between us to your two daughters. Let me hear how it affects each of them towards me. Let me know what they are willing to think and ready to do under such unparalleled circumstances as have now occurred. I will wait *your* time, and *their* time; I will abide by *your* decision and *their* decision, pronounced after the first poignant distress and irritation of this day's events have passed over.'

Still Mr Langley remained silent; the angry word was on his tongue; the contemptuous rejection of what he regarded for the moment as a proposition equally ill-timed and insolent, seemed bursting to his lips; but once more he restrained himself. He rose from his seat, and walked slowly backwards and forwards, deep in thought. Mr Streatfield was too much overcome by his own agitation to plead his cause further by another word. There was a silence in the room now, which lasted for some time.

We have said that Mr Langley was a man of the world. He was strongly attached to his children; but he had a little of the selfishness and much of the reverence for wealth of a man of the world. As he now endeavoured to determine mentally on his proper course of action—to disentangle the whole case from all its mysterious intricacies—to view it, extraordinary as it was, in its proper bearings, his thoughts began gradually to assume what is called 'a practical turn'. He reflected that he had another daughter, besides the twin sisters, to provide for; and that he had two sons to settle in life. He was not rich enough to portion three daughters; and he had not interest enough to start his sons favourably in a career of eminence. Mr Streatfield, on the contrary, was a man of great wealth, and of great 'connections' among people in power. Was such a son-in-law to be rejected, even after all that had happened, without at least consulting his wife and daughters first? He thought not. Had not Mr Streatfield, in truth, been the victim of a remarkable fatality, of an incredible accident, and were no allowances, under such circumstances, to be made for him? He began to think there were. Reflecting thus, he determined at length to proceed with moderation and caution at all hazards; and regained composure enough to continue the conversation in a cold, but still in a polite tone.

'I will commit myself, sir, to no agreement or promise whatever,' he began, 'nor will I consider this interview in any respect as a conclusive one, either on your side or mine; but if I think, on consideration, that it is desirable that our conversation should be repeated to my wife and daughters, I will make them acquainted with it, and will let you know the result. In the meantime, I think you will agree with me, that it is most fit that the next communications between us should take place by letter alone.'

Mr Streatfield was not slow in taking the hint conveyed by Mr Langley's last words. After what had occurred, and until something was definitely settled, he felt that the suffering and suspense which he was already enduring would be increased tenfold if he remained longer in the same house with the twin sisters—the betrothed of one, the lover of the other! Murmuring a few inaudible words of acquiescence in the arrangements which had just been proposed to him, he left the room. The same evening he quitted Langley Hall.

The next morning the remainder of the guests departed, their curiosity to know all the particulars of what had happened remaining ungratified. They were simply informed that an extraordinary and unexpected obstacle had arisen to delay the wedding; that no blame attached to any one in the matter; and that as soon as everything had been finally determined, everything would be explained. Until then, it was not considered necessary to enter in any way into particulars. By the middle of the day every visitor had left the house; and a strange and melancholy spectacle it presented when they were all gone. Rooms were now empty and silent, which the day before had been filled with animated groups, and had echoed with merry laughter. In one apartment, the fittings for the series of tableaux which had been proposed remained half completed: the dresses that were to have been worn lay scattered on the floor; the carpenter who had come to proceed with his work gathered up his tools in ominous silence, and departed as quickly as he could. Here lay books still open at the last page read; there was an album, with the drawing of the day before unfinished, and the colour box unclosed by its side. On the deserted billiard-table, the positions of the 'cues' and balls showed traces of an interrupted game. Flowers were scattered on the rustic tables in the garden, half-made into nosegays, and beginning to wither already. The very dogs wandered in a moody, unsettled way about the house, missing the friendly hands that had fondled and fed them for so many days past, and whining impatiently in the deserted drawing rooms. The social desolation of the scene was miserably complete in all its aspects.

Immediately after the departure of his guests, Mr Langley had a long interview with his wife. He repeated to her the conversation which had taken place between Mr Streatfield and himself, and received from her in return such an account of the conduct of his daughter, under the trial that had befallen her, as filled him with equal astonishment and admiration. It was a new revelation to him of the character of his own child.

'As soon as the violent symptoms had subsided,' said Mrs Langley, in answer to her husband's first inquiries, 'as soon as the hysterical fit was subdued, Jane seemed suddenly to assume a new character, to become another person. She begged that the doctor might be released from his attendance, and that she might be left alone with me and with her sister Clara. When every one else had quitted the room, she continued to sit in the easy chair where we had at first placed her, covering her face with her hands. She entreated us not to speak to her for a short time, and, except that she shuddered occasionally, sat quite still and silent. When she at last looked up, we were shocked to see the deadly paleness of her face, and the strange alteration that had come over her expression; but she spoke to us so coherently, so solemnly even, that we were amazed; we knew not what to think or what to do; it hardly seemed to be *our* Jane who was now speaking to us.'

'What did she say?' asked Mr Langley, eagerly.

'She said that the first feeling of her heart, at that moment, was gratitude on her own account. She thanked God that the terrible discovery had not been made too late, when her married life might have been a life of estrangement and misery. Up to the moment when Mr Streatfield had uttered that one fatal exclamation, she had loved him, she told us, fondly and fervently; *now*, no explanation, no repentance (if either were tendered), no earthly persuasion or command (in case Mr Streatfield should think himself bound, as a matter of atonement, to hold to his rash engagement), could ever induce her to become his wife.'

'Mr Streatfield will not test her resolution,' said Mr Langley, bitterly; 'he deliberately repeated his repudiation of his engagement in this room; nay, more, he—'

'I have something important to say to you from Jane on this point,' interrupted Mrs Langley. 'After she had spoken the first few words which I have already repeated to you, she told us that she had been thinking—thinking more calmly perhaps than we could imagine—on all that had happened; on what Mr Streatfield had said at the dinner table; on the momentary glance of recognition which she had seen pass between him and her sister Clara, whose accidental absence, during the whole period of Mr Streatfield's intercourse with us in London, she now remembered and reminded me of. The cause of the fatal error, and the manner in which it had occurred, seemed to be already known to her, as if by intuition. We entreated her to refrain from speaking on the subject for the present; but she answered that it was her duty to speak on it—her duty to propose something which should alleviate the suspense and distress we were all enduring on her account. No words can describe to you her fortitude, her noble endurance—' Mrs Langley's voice faltered as she pronounced the last words. It was some minutes ere she became sufficiently composed to proceed thus:

'I am charged with a message to you from Jane—I should say, charged with her entreaties, that you will not suspend our intercourse with Mr Streatfield, or view his conduct in any other than a merciful light—as conduct for which accident and circumstances are alone to blame. After she had given me this message to you, she turned to Clara, who sat weeping by her side, completely overcome; and kissing her, said that *they* were to blame, if anyone was to be blamed in the matter, for being so much alike as to make all who saw them apart doubt which was Clara and which was Jane. She said this with a faint smile, and an effort to speak playfully, which touched us to the heart. Then, in a tone and manner which I can never forget, she asked her sister—charging her, on their mutual affection and mutual confidence, to answer sincerely—if *she* had noticed Mr Streatfield on the day of the levée, and afterwards remembered him at the dinner table, as *he* had noticed and remembered *her*? It was only after Jane had repeated this appeal, still more earnestly and affectionately, that Clara summoned courage and composure enough to confess that she *had* noticed Mr Streatfield on the day of the levée, had thought of him afterwards during her absence from London, and had recognized him at our table, as he had recognized her.'

'Is it possible! I own I had not anticipated—not thought for one moment of that,' said Mr Langley.

'Perhaps,' continued his wife, 'it is best that you should see Jane now, and judge for yourself. For *my* part, her noble resignation under this great trial has so astonished and impressed me that I only feel competent to advise as she advises, to act as she thinks fit. I begin to think that it is not *we* who are to guide *her*, but *she* who is to guide *us.*'

Mr Langley lingered irresolute for a few minutes; then quitted the room, and proceeded alone to Jane Langley's apartment.

When he knocked at the door, it was opened by Clara. There was an expression partly of confusion, partly of sorrow on her face; and when her father stopped as if to speak to her, she merely pointed into the room, and hurried away without uttering a word.

Mr Langley had been prepared by his wife for the change that had taken place in his daughter since the day before; but he felt startled, almost overwhelmed, as he now looked on her. One of the poor girl's most prominent attractions, from her earliest years, had been the beauty of her complexion; and now, the freshness and the bloom had entirely departed from her face; it seemed absolutely colourless. Her expression, too, appeared to Mr Langley's eyes to have undergone a melancholy alteration; to have lost its youthfulness suddenly; to have assumed a strange character of firmness and thoughtfulness, which he had never observed in it before. She was sitting by an open window, commanding a lovely view of wide, sunny landscape; a Bible which her mother had given her, lay open on her knees; she was reading it as her father entered. For the first time in his life, he paused, speechless, as he approached to speak to one of his own children.

'I am afraid I look very ill,' she said, holding out her hand to him; 'but I am better than I look; I shall be quite well in a day or two. Have you heard my message, father? Have you been told?'

'My love, we will not speak of it yet; we will wait a few days,' said Mr Langley.

'You have always been so kind to me,' she continued, in less steady tones, 'that I am sure you will let me go on. I have very little to say, but that little must be said now, and then we need never recur to it again. Will you consider all that has happened as something forgotten? You have heard already what it is I entreat you to do; will you let *him*—Mr Streatfield—' (She stopped, her voice failed for a moment, but she recovered herself again almost immediately.) 'Will you let Mr Streatfield remain here, or recall him if he is gone, and give him an opportunity of explaining himself to my sister? If poor Clara should refuse to see him for my sake, pray do not listen to her. I am sure this is what ought to be done; I have been thinking of it very calmly, and I feel that it is right. And there is something more I have to beg of you, father; it is that, while Mr Streatfield is here, you will allow me to go and stay with my aunt. You know how fond she is of me. Her house is not a day's journey from home. It is best for everybody (much the best for *me*) that I should not remain here at present; and—and—dear father! I have always been your spoiled child; and I know you will indulge me still. If you do what I ask you, I shall soon get over this heavy trial. I shall be well again if I am away at my aunt's—if—'

She paused; and putting one trembling arm around her father's neck, hid her face on his breast. For some minutes, Mr Langley could not trust himself to answer her. There was something, not deeply touching only, but impressive and sublime, about the moral heroism of this young girl, whose heart and mind—hitherto wholly inexperienced in the harder and darker emergencies of life—now rose in the strength of their native purity superior to the bitterest, cruellest trial that either could undergo; whose patience and resignation, called forth for the first time by a calamity which suddenly thwarted the purposes and paralysed the affections that had been destined to endure for a life, could thus appear at once in the fullest maturity of virtue and beauty. As the father thought on these things; as he vaguely and imperfectly estimated the extent of the daughter's sacrifice; as he reflected on the nature of the affliction that had befallen her—which combined in itself a fatality that none could have foreseen, a fault that could neither be repaired nor resented, a judgement against which there was no appeal—and then remembered how this affliction had been borne, with what words and what actions it had been met, he felt that it would be almost a profanation to judge the touching petition just addressed to him, by the criterion of *his* worldly doubts and *his* worldly wisdom. His eye fell on the Bible, still open beneath it; he remembered the little child who was set in the midst of the disciples, as teacher and example to all; and when at length he spoke in answer to his daughter, it was not to direct or to advise, but to comfort and comply.

They delayed her removal for a few days, to see if she faltered in her resolution, if her bodily weakness increased; but she never wavered; nothing in her appearance changed, either for better or for worse. A week after the startling scene at the dinner table, she was living in the strictest retirement in the house of her aunt.

About the period of her departure, a letter was received from Mr Streatfield. It was little more than a recapitulation of what he had already said to Mr Langley—expressed, however, on this occasion, in stronger and, at the same time, in more respectful terms. The letter was answered briefly; he was informed that nothing had, as yet, been determined on, but that the next communication would bring him a final reply.

Two months passed. During that time, Jane Langley was frequently visited at her aunt's house by her father and mother. She still remained calm and resolved; still looked pale and thoughtful, as at first. Doctors were consulted: they talked of a shock to the nervous system; of great hope from time, and their patient's strength of mind; and of the necessity of acceding to her wishes in all things. Then, the advice of the aunt was sought. She was a woman of an eccentric, masculine character, who had herself experienced a love disappointment in early life, and had never married. She gave her opinion unreservedly and abruptly, as she always gave it. 'Do as Jane tells you!' said the old lady, severely; 'that poor child has more moral courage and determination than all the rest of you put together! I know better than anybody what a sacrifice she has had to make; but she has made it; and made it nobly—like a heroine, as some people would say; like a good, high-minded, courageous girl, as *I* say! Do as she tells you! Let that poor, selfish fool of a man have his way, and marry her sister—he has made one mistake already about a face—see if he doesn't find out, some day, that he has made another, about a wife! Let him!—Jane is too good for *him*, or for any man! Leave her to me; let her stop here; she shan't lose by what has happened! You know this place is mine—I mean it to be hers, when I'm dead. You know I've got some money—I shall leave it to her. I've made my will: it's all done and settled! Go back home; send for the man, and tell Clara to marry him without any more fuss! You wanted my opinion—there it is for you!'

At last Mr Langley decided. The important letter was written, which recalled Mr Streatfield to Langley Hall. As Jane had foreseen, Clara at first refused to hold any communication with him; but a letter from her sister, and the remonstrances of her father, soon changed her resolution. There was nothing in common between the twin sisters but their personal resemblance. Clara had been guided all her life by the opinions of others, and she was guided by them now.

Once permitted the opportunity of pleading his cause, Mr Streatfield did not neglect his own interests. It would be little to our purpose to describe the doubts and difficulties which delayed at first the progress of his second courtship—pursued as it was under circumstances, not only extraordinary, but unprecedented. It is no longer, with him, or with Clara Langley, that the interest of our story is connected. Suffice it to say, that he ultimately overcame all the young lady's scruples; and that, a few months afterwards, some of Mr Langley's intimate friends found themselves again assembled round his table as wedding guests, and congratulating Mr Streatfield on his approaching union with Clara, as they had already congratulated him, scarcely a year back, on his approaching union with Jane!

The social ceremonies of the wedding day were performed soberly—almost sadly. Some of the guests (especially the unmarried ladies) thought that Miss Clara had allowed herself to be won too easily—others were picturing to themselves the situation of the poor girl who was absent; and contributed little towards the gaiety of the party. On this occasion, however, nothing occurred to interrupt the proceedings; the marriage took place; and, immediately after it, Mr Streatfield and his bride started for a tour on the Continent.

On their departure, Jane Langley returned home. She made no reference whatever to her sister's marriage; and no one mentioned it in her presence. Still the colour did not return to her cheek, or the old gaiety to her manner. The shock that she had suffered had left its traces on her for life. But there was no evidence that she was sinking under the remembrances which neither time nor resolution could banish. The strong, pure heart had undergone a change, but not a deterioration. All that had been brilliant in her character was gone; but all that was noble in it remained. Never had her intercourse with her family and her friends been so affectionate and so kindly as it was now.

When, after a long absence, Mr Streatfield and his wife returned to England, it was observed, at her first meeting with them, that the momentary confusion and embarrassment were on *their* side, not on *hers*. During their stay at Langley Hall, she showed not the slightest disposition to avoid them. No member of the family welcomed them more cordially; entered into all their plans and projects more readily; or bade them farewell with a kinder or better grace, when they departed for their own home.

Our tale is nearly ended: what remains of it must comprise the history of many years in the compass of a few words.

Time passed on; and Death and Change told of its lapse among the family at Langley Hall. Five years after the events above related, Mr Langley died; and was followed to the grave, shortly afterwards, by his wife. Of their two sons, the eldest was rising into good practice at the bar; the youngest had become attaché to a foreign embassy. Their third daughter was married, and living at the family seat of her husband, in Scotland. Mr and Mrs Streatfield had children of their own, now, to occupy their time and absorb their care. The career of life was over for some—the purposes of life had altered for others—Jane Langley alone still remained unchanged.

She now lived entirely with her aunt. At intervals—as their worldly duties and worldly avocations permitted them—the other members of her family, or one or two intimate friends, came to the house. Offers of marriage were made to her, but were all declined. The first, last love of her girlish days—abandoned as a hope, and crushed as a passion; living only as a quiet grief, as a pure remembrance—still kept its watch, as guardian and defender, over her heart. Years passed on and worked no change in the sad uniformity of her life, until the death of her aunt left her mistress of the house in which she had hitherto been a guest. Then it was observed that she made fewer and fewer efforts to vary the tenor of existence, to forget her old remembrances for awhile in the society of others. Such invitations as reached her from relations and friends were more frequently declined than accepted. She was growing old herself now; and, with each advancing year, the busy pageant of the outer world presented less and less that could attract her eye.

So she began to surround herself, in her solitude, with the favourite books that she had studied, with the favourite music that she had played, in the days of her hopes and her happiness. Everything that was associated, however slightly, with that past period, now acquired a character of inestimable value in her eyes, as aiding her mind to seclude itself more and more strictly in the sanctuary of its early recollections. Was it weakness in her to live thus; to abandon the world and the world's interests, as one who had no hope, or part in either? Had she earned the right, by the magnitude and resolution of her sacrifice, thus to indulge in the sad luxury of fruitless remembrance? Who shall say!—who shall presume to decide that cannot think with *her* thoughts, and look back with *her* recollections!

Thus she lived—alone, and yet not lonely; without hope, but with no despair; separate and apart from the world around her, except when she approached it by her charities to the poor, and her succour to the afflicted; by her occasional interviews with the surviving members of her family and a few old friends, when they sought her in her calm retreat; and by little presents which she constantly sent to brothers' and sisters' children, who worshipped, as their invisible good genius, 'the kind lady' whom most of them had never seen. Such was her existence throughout the closing years of her life: such did it continue—calm and blameless—to the last.

Reader, when you are told that what is impressive and pathetic in the Drama of Human Life has passed with a past age of Chivalry and Romance, remember Jane Langley, and quote in contradiction the story of the TWIN SISTERS!

8

THE LAST STAGE COACHMAN

The Last Stage Coachman! It falls upon the ear of every one but a shareholder in railways, with a boding, melancholy sound. In spite of our natural reverence for the wonders of science, our hearts grow heavy at the thought of never again beholding the sweet-smelling nosegay, the unimpeachable top boots, and fair white breeches; once so prominent as the uniform of the fraternity. With all our respect for expeditious and business-like travelling, we experience a feeling nearly akin to disgust at being marshalled to our places by a bell and a fellow with a badge on his shoulder; instead of hearing the cheery summons, 'Now then, gentlemen,' and being regaled by a short and instructive conversation with a ruddy-faced personage in a dustless olive-green coat and prismatic belcher handkerchief. What did we want with smoke? Had we not the coachman's cigar, if we were desirous of observing its shapes and appearances? Who would be so unreasonable as to languish for steam, when he could inhale it on a cool, autumnal morning, naturally concocted from the backs of four blood horses? Who!—Alas! we may propose questions and find out answers to the end of the chapter, and yet fail in reforming the perverted taste of the present generation; we know that the attempt is useless, and we give up in sorrowful and philosophic resignation, and proceed undaunted by the probable sneers of railway directors, to the recital of—

A Vision.

Methought I walked forth one autumn evening to observe the arrival of a stage coach. I wandered on, yet nothing of the kind met my eye. I tried many an old public road—they were now grass-grown and miry, or desecrated by the abominable presence of a 'station'. I wended my way towards a famous roadside inn: it was desolate and silent, or in other words, 'To Let'. I looked for 'the commercial room': not a pot of beer adorned the mouldering tables, and not a pipe lay scattered over the wild and beautiful seclusions of its once numerous 'boxes'. It was deserted and useless; the voice of the traveller rung no longer round its walls, and the merry horn of the guard startled no more the sleepy few, who once congregated round its hospitable door. The chill fireplace and broad, antiquated mantelpiece presented but one bill—the starting time of an adjacent railroad; surmounted by a representation of those engines of destruction, in dull, frowsy lithograph.

I turned to the yard. Where was the ostler with his unbraced breeches and his upturned shirtsleeves? Where was the stableboy with his wisp of straw and his sieve of oats? Where were the coquettish mares and the tall blood horses? Where was the manger and the stable door?—All gone—all disappeared: the buildings dilapidated and tottering—of what use is a stable to a stoker? The ostler and stableboy had passed away—what fellowship have either with a boiler? *The inn yard was no more!* The very dunghill in its farthest corner was choked by dust and old bricks, and the cock, the pride of the country round, clamoured no longer on the ruined and unsightly wall. I thought it was possible that he had satisfied long since the cravings of a railway committee; and I sat down on a ruined water-tub to give way to the melancholy reflections called up by the sight before me.

I know not how long I meditated. There was no officious waiter to ask me, 'What I would please to order?' No chambermaid to simper out, 'This way, Sir,'—not even a stray cat to claim acquaintance with the calves of my legs, or a horse's hoof to tread upon my toe. There was nothing to disturb my miserable reverie, and I anathematized railways without distinction or exception.

The distant sound of slow and stealthy footsteps at last attracted my attention. I looked to the far end of the yard. Heavens above! a stage coachman was pacing its worn and weedy pavement.

There was no mistaking him—he wore the low-crowned, broad-brimmed, whitey-brown, well-brushed hat; the voluminous checked neckcloth; the ample-skirted coat; the striped waistcoat; the white cords; and last, not least, the immortal boots. But alas! the calf that had once filled them out had disappeared; they clanked heavily on the pavement, instead of creaking tightly and noisily wherever he went. His waistcoat, evidently once filled almost to bursting, hung in loose, uncomfortable folds about his emaciated waist: large wrinkles marred the former beauty of the fit of his coat: and his face was all lines and furrows, instead of smiles and jollity. The spirit of the fraternity had passed away from him—he was the stage coachman only in dress.

He walked backwards and forwards for some time without turning his head one way or the other, except now and then to peer into the deserted stable, or to glance mournfully at the whip he held in his hand: at last the sound of the arrival of a train struck upon his ear!

He drew himself up to his full height, slowly and solemnly shook his clenched fist in the direction of the sound, and looked—Oh that look! it spoke annihilation to the mightiest engine upon the rail, it scoffed at steam, and flashed furious derision at the largest terminus that ever was erected; it was an awfully comprehensive look—the concentrated essence of the fierce and deadly enmity of all the stage coachmen in England to steam conveyance.

To my utter astonishment, not, it must be owned, unmixed with fear, he suddenly turned his eyes towards my place of shelter, and walked up to me.

'That's the rail,' said he, between his set teeth.

'It is,' said I, considerably embarrassed.

'Damn it!' returned the excited Stage Coachman.

There was something inexpressibly awful about this execration; and I confess I felt a strong internal conviction that the next day's paper would teem with horrible railway accidents in every column.

'I did my utmost to hoppose 'em,' said the Stage Coachman, in softened accents. 'I wos the *last* that guv' in, I kep' a losing day after day, and yet I worked on; I wos determined to do my dooty, and I drove a coach the last day with an old hooman and a carpet bag inside, and three little boys and seven whopping empty portmanteaus outside. I wos determined my last kick to have *some* passengers to show to the rail, so I took my wife and children cos nobody else wouldn't go, and then we guv' in. Hows'ever, the last time as *I* wos on the road I didn't go and show 'em an empty coach—we wasn't full, but we wasn't empty; we wos game to the last!'

A grim smile of triumph lit up the features of the deposed Coachman as he gave vent to this assertion. He took hold of me by the buttonhole, and led the way into the house.

'This landlord wos an austerious sort of a man,' said he; 'he used to hobserve that he only wished a Railway Committee would dine at his house, he'd pison 'em all, and emigrate; and he'd ha' done it, too!'

I did not venture to doubt this, so the stage coachman continued:

'I've smoked my pipe by the hour together in that fireplace; I've read *The Times* adwertisements and Perlice Reports in that box till I fell asleep; I've walked up and down this here room a-saying all sorts of things about the rail, and a-busting for happiness. Outside this wery door I've bin a-drownded in thankys from ladies for never lettin' nobody step through their bandboxes. The chambermaids used to smile, and the dogs used to bark, wherever I came.—But it's all hover now—the poor feller as kep' this place takes tickets at a Station, and the chambermaids makes scalding hot tea behind a mahuggany counter for people as has no time to drink it in!'

As the Stage Coachman uttered these words, a contemptuous sneer puckered his sallow cheek. He led me back into the yard; the ruined appearance of which looked doubly mournful, under the faint rays of moonlight that every here and there stole through the dilapidated walls of the stable. An owl had taken up his abode, where the chief ostler's bedroom had once rejoiced in the grotesque majesty of huge portraits of every winner of every 'Derby', since the first days of Epsom. The bird of night flew heavily off at our approach, and my companion pointed gloomily up to the fragments of mouldy, worm-eaten wood, the last relics of the stable loft.

'He wos a great friend of mine, was that h'ostler,' said the Coachman, 'but he's left this railway-bothered world—he was finished by the train.'

At my earnest entreaty to hear further, he continued:

'When this h'old place, wos guv' up and ruinated; the h'ostler as 'ud never look at the rail before went down to have a sight of it, and as he wos a-leaning his elbows on the wall, and a-wishing as how he had the stabling of all the steam h'ingines (he'd ha' done 'em justice!), wot should he see, but one of his 'osses as wos thrown out of employ by the rail, awalking along jist where the train was coming. Bill jumped down, and as he wos aleading of him h'off, up comes the train, and went over his leg and cut the 'oss in two—"Tom," says he to me when we picked him up; "I'm agoing eleven mile an hour, to the last stage as is left for me to do. I've always done my dooty with the 'osses; I've bin and done it now—bury that ere poor 'oss and me out of the noise of the rail." We got the surgeons to him, but he never spoke no more, Poor Bill! Poor Bill!'

This last recollection seemed too much for the Stage Coachman; he wrung my hand, and walked abruptly to the furthest corner of the yard.

I took care not to interrupt him, and watched him carefully from a distance.

At first, the one expression of his countenance was melancholy; but by degrees, other thoughts came crowding from his mind, and mantled on his woebegone visage. Poor fellow, I could see that he was again in imagination the beloved of the ladies and the adored of the chambermaids: a faint reflection of the affable, yet majestic demeanour, required by his calling, flitted occasionally over his pinched, attenuated features; and brightened the cold, melancholy expression of his countenance.

As I still looked, it grew darker and darker, yet the face of the Stage Coachman was never for an instant hidden from me. The same artificial expression of pleasure characterized its lineaments as before. Suddenly I heard a strange, unnatural noise in the air—now it seemed like the distant trampling of horses; and now again, like the rumbling of a heavily laden coach along a public road. A faint, sickly light spread itself over that part of the Heavens whence the sounds proceeded; and after an interval, a fully equipped Stage Coach appeared in the clouds, with a railway director strapped fast to each wheel, and a stoker between the teeth of each of the four horses.

In place of luggage, fragments of broken steam carriages, and red carpet bags, filled with other mementos of railway accidents, occupied the roof. Chance passengers appeared to be the only tenants of the outside places. In front sat Julius Caesar and Mrs Hannah Moore; and behind, Sir Joseph Banks and Mrs Brownrigge. Of all the 'insides', I could, I grieve to say, see nothing.

On the box was a little man with fuzzy hair and large iron-grey whiskers; clothed in a coat of engineers' skin, with gloves of the hide of railway police. He pulled up opposite my friend, and bowing profoundly motioned him to the box seat.

A gleam of unutterable joy irradiated the Stage Coachman's countenance, as he stepped lightly into his place, seized the reins, and with one hearty 'good-night', addressed to an imaginary inn-full of people, started the horses.

Off they drove! my friend in the plenitude of his satisfaction cracking the whip every instant as he drove the phantom coach into the air. And amidst the shrieks of the railway directors at the wheel, the groans of James Watt, the bugle of the guard, and the tremendous cursing of the invisible 'insides', fast and furiously disappeared from my eyes.

ABOUT TERRY O'BRIEN

Terry O'Brien is an academic with three decades of experience in teaching language and communication skills in India and abroad. He also headed a college under the auspices of the University of Delhi.

A prolific writer, with several books to his credit, Terry O'Brien is a reputed professional motivational speaker and a quizmaster.